Copyright © 2021 Brianna Skylark

All rights reserved.

ISBN-13: 9781080921034

This is a work of fiction. Names, characters, places, and incidents either are the product of the author's imagination or are used fictitiously. Any resemblance to actual persons, living or dead, events, or locales is entirely coincidental.

Copyright © 2019 by Brianna Skylark.

All rights reserved. No part of this publication may be reproduced, distributed, or transmitted in any form or by any means, including photocopying, recording, or other electronic or mechanical methods, including information storage and retrieval systems, without the prior written permission of the author, except in the case of brief quotations embodied in critical reviews and certain other noncommercial uses permitted by copyright law.

First edition July 2019.

www.briannaskylark.com

BE WITH US

An Urban Foursome Love Story

BRIANNA SKYLARK

*

Be With Us: An Urban Foursome Love Story is the first book in the **Erotic Swingers** series and is followed by **Play With Us: An Urban Foursome Game Night Fantasy**. The third book in the series is **Come With Us: An Urban Foursome Vacation Romance**. The fourth and final book is **Stay With Us: An Urban Foursome Swingers Ménage.** The companion novel **The Paramour: A Romantic Victorian Ménage** is also

Be With Us

available to read.

Two hot couples, one skin-tingling night of passion...

Blissfully married **bombshell Emilia** has never been with anyone but her **rugged high-school sweetheart Cass.**

He's confident, strong, dark and handsome, and **he's all hers**... but innocent Emilia has a **burning desire**. She wants to be touched and kissed, and held... and **shared**, in every imaginable way.

So when their hearts are **tempted** by **fiery redhead Amy** and her **dominant bodyguard husband Mark** at a decadent masquerade ball, lust turns into infatuation and an unexpected crush creates heartache and jealously, complicating an exhilarating new friendship.

Will opening up their perfect marriage be a step too far? Or will it be a journey of sexual awakening that will transform their lives forever...

Now a series of five deliciously naughty novels, filled with saucy swinger fun, and filthy forbidden romance.

Stories by Brianna Skylark

Erotic Swingers

Be With Us - An Urban Foursome Love Story

Play With Us - An Urban Foursome Game Night Fantasy

Come With Us - An Urban Foursome Vacation Romance

Stay With Us - An Urban Foursome Swingers Ménage

The Paramour - An Erotic Victorian Ménage

Fantasy Swingers

Tushie - A Taboo Tale of Forbidden Love

Muffin - A First Time FFM Ménage Romance

Bootie - A Hotwife Fantasy MFM Ménage

Cupcake - A Wife Swap Swingers Tale

Peach - A Penthouse Swingers Party

Petal - A Swingers Vacation Fantasy

Pumpkin - A Halloween Mystery Ménage

Precious - A Wedding Swingers Fantasy

Snowdrop - A Secret Santa Wife Swap

The Billionaire's Naked Cleaner

Sweet and Discreet - Confessions of a Naked Cleaner

Sparkle and Spice - Adventures of a Naked Cleaner

Squeaky and Clean - Affairs of a Naked Cleaner

Naughty and Nice - Envy of a Naked Cleaner

Stars and Shine - Romance of a Naked Cleaner

First Time Swingers

Into the Swing - A First Time Wife Swap Fantasy

Back Swing - A Truth or Dare Swingers Fantasy

Hot Swing - A Hot Tub Swingers Fantasy

Mistletoe Swing - A Christmas Wife Swap Fantasy

Little Swing - An MFM Lockdown Ménage

Power Swing - A Billionaire Swingers Fantasy

Cyber Swing - A Swipe Right Wife Swap Fantasy

Jingle Swing - A Christmas Foursome Fantasy

Strip Swing - A Best Friends Striptease Foursome

Dark Swing - A Desert Biker Wife Swap Fantasy

Forbidden Temptations

Throwback - An Enemies to Lovers Fantasy

Fifth Base - A Cheeky First Time Fantasy

Other Books

Sharing Rose - A Romantic MFM Mountain Ménage

CHAPTER ONE

The afternoon sun shone down a little too warm as Emilia relaxed on the wooden lounger in her back garden. Her sandals were off, her feet were stretched out, her toes were pointed, and her legs were ever so slightly apart.

Half an hour prior she had returned home from her shift at the city hospital, swiftly changing into a short floaty skirt and a shoestring camisole top. She'd thought about her outfit very carefully, and had done so for days in anticipation of this moment, and as a result, she was feeling very kinky, her naughty thoughts sending little shivers of arousal travelling throughout her body like sparkles of electricity, for this was to be no *ordinary* afternoon.

It was spring, and it was quiet. Occasionally she could hear the sound of bluebirds flitting between the branches of the cluster of trees that bordered their fence, the only barrier between her and the normally busy road beyond. She listened nervously and felt a small tingle of apprehension, her chest

Chapter One

thumping as next door's patio door slid open, closely followed by the quiet footsteps of Josie, their mousy and friendly neighbour as she made her way into her own garden. After a few tense moments, Emilia could make out the snip-snip of shears as she began to tend to her roses and her stomach filled with trepidation.

Could she really do this?

She'd been thinking about her risqué plan for a while, indecorously inspired after she'd read a racy scene in her favourite naughty book, an idea that had tickled her in places she'd thought long dormant, and she had finally managed to build up the courage to see what... *it* would feel like.

She took a deep breath.

Her husband wouldn't be home for an hour, so she had plenty of time. But now, faced with the prospect of actually carrying out her plan, she was starting to feel silly and somewhat on edge. If she didn't do it now, she thought to herself with a little tingle of excitement, then she might never have the courage to try it again.

She lay still, savouring the anticipation and then ever so delicately, she rolled up the edge of her top, laying her hands flat on her stomach and spreading out her fingers, before looking around as she lightly traced the contour of her belly. Tingling with the thrill of the moment, she picked up her battered novel from the decking and flicked it open.

It was already on the right page.

Her sister, Alice had recommended this book to her over a year ago. Emilia had initially baulked at the idea of reading an erotic Victorian romance, particularly the kind that she was now cradling in her palms, but the seed had been planted in a wholly repressed and mortifyingly shameful part of her mind, and there it had *blossomed*, and as she had become more and more curious she had *shamefully* agreed to borrow it, but instead, her sister had *gifted* her, her very own copy.

The Paramour was set in the lonely highlands of Scotland and centred on the unconventional love between the Duke, the Duchess Elizabeth and her best friend, Lady Victoria. And it was *so naughty*. She had read it so many times now that it could only be regarded as ruined, battered and crinkled - *a book no more* - instead it had become a totem of shame.

Beautiful, sexy, *shame*.

She had read this particular chapter so many times that she knew it almost by *heart*, often recounting a little of it under her breath during quiet moments on her shifts whilst she tried not to blush. Usually out of earshot of the other medical staff and her patients.

Usually.

It wasn't just the thought of the book that had inflamed her, not entirely. It was the thought of what she planned to do to *herself* as she read it.

That was the exciting part.

Every two weeks she and her husband Cassian's work patterns left her with a whole hour on her lonesome - a *happy* hour so to speak - and she would often come home, sneak up to their bedroom and have a little sensual *alone* time, and this week was no exception… except this week she was going to have a little fun *outside*, with the sun warming her face.

But that wasn't all of it, not if she was honest.

What had aroused her so much, was the thought that one of her *neighbours* in the houses that overlooked their garden might, maybe, just a little bit… glance down from a first-floor window or peek quietly through a hole in the fence and *see* her.

Oh gosh, she thought as she closed her eyes.

It was the taboo thought of being watched as she *touched* herself; a willing participant in an act of

Chapter One

voyeurism that had inflamed her so, and every good-girl part of her body was horrified at the thought.

She was turned on by the fear and the guilt of being *caught*.

And it was making her feel shockingly giddy, and unmentionably aroused.

She'd never done it outside before and for weeks since the idea had fomented in her mind, she had found herself feeling like a young girl again, discovering her body for the first time. She'd never touched herself beyond the confines of her own *bedroom* before, and for an inordinate amount of time each day, the idea had been preoccupying her thoughts.

Deep breath.

She tried and failed to settle herself down and then slowly she began to read, her breathing already uneven and shallow, her hands and fingers trembling.

Snip snip went Josie's shears.

The Duke was stood by the hearth of the manor, stoking a roaring fire which blazed from the coals as a storm swept down through the moor and battered the old stone building, whilst on the chaise-longe opposite him, huddled under a thick blanket were the wet-through figures of the Lady and the Duchess, stripped down to their underclothes, warming themselves before the roaring flames.

You can do this, she breathed.

As she read, she carefully slipped the tips of her fingers underneath the waistband of her skirt and into her knickers, and took a long, deep and stuttering breath, as *skin touched skin*.

Oh gosh.

She started slow, circling herself surreptitiously with a single fingertip, her movements steady and subtle, whilst her eyes flicked up and around guiltily before finding the pages once more.

She read on as *Elizabeth stroked Victoria's knuckles beneath the large blanket, and then ever so delicately moved her hand down to her friend's naked thigh.* She closed her eyes, picturing the scene, whilst running her wet fingers down to her opening and back up to her clit.

Beneath the blanket by the fire, the shy and retiring Victoria had found herself electrified at the touch of her friend, and after some gentle exploration was now slowly unlacing Elizabeth's petticoat strings as her hands explored between Victoria's thighs.

Emilia quickened her pace, pushing her fingers inside and arching her head back, her eyes closed as she pleasured herself.

Oh wow.

The book fell aside, but it didn't matter, she knew the story well enough that she didn't need it. She pictured Elizabeth's fingers making their way up Victoria's thigh, finding the edge of her undergarments and slipping inside them. She saw in her mind as the Duke stood up and made his way over to the two women, throwing aside the rug and revealing their secret and illicit affair, and her fingers swirled faster.

Her underwear was getting wet and she pushed it down past her bottom and let out a quiet involuntary moan, and then she blushed and froze as she wondered if Josie might've heard.

Snip sni-

Her heart thumped in her chest.

As she started again, she found she was picturing herself as Lady Victoria, as the strong arms of the Duke picked her up and handled her like a doll, positioning her against the tall edge of the chaise-longe, his trousers falling aside and his thick member searching and then *slipping* into her from behind.

Emilia's fingers were deep inside herself now, her movements no longer subtle or quiet, if anyone was looking

Chapter One

out of their window they would see her playing with herself, and the thought made her quicken. She felt herself beginning to climax, her eyes fluttering open and looking around anxiously as her mouth let out another soft moan. Her fingers worked quickly against her clit, and for a fleeting moment, she thought she heard Cassian calling her name.

She suddenly felt ashamed and guilty at the thought of her husband catching her thinking about another man - *and another woman* - her fingers between her thighs. Then to her surprise, she felt a sudden rush of arousal as she pictured him in the room with them, seeing her bent over the chair, the Duke thrusting into her and filling her with his seed, knowing that Cassian would be next in line to have her, to *claim* her.

The thought of him watching her with the Duke caught her off guard and she felt a blush rise up past her neck as her whole body quivered, then her spine arched and her mouth fell open and she started to come, holding her breath, her fingers *deep* inside her pussy… and then she *could* hear Cassian calling for her.

He was in the house, he had come home early, but it was too late - she had passed the point of no return.

She gripped the edge of the wooden lounger as she shuddered in climax, desperately trying to stifle the moan escaping her lips, her mouth wide and her eyes screwed shut as she bent forward and bucked hard.

Now the conservatory door was opening and she could hear him stepping onto the decking as she collapsed back down onto the lounger, her fingers still inside herself, twitching and pulsing as she gasped for breath.

'Em, you okay?' he said. 'You asleep?'

'*Huh?*' she managed, her chest still shaking from the intensity of her orgasm. Her lips and tongue were dry and she was breathing erratically as she rolled away sideways and slid her hand back out of her skirt, smoothing herself down and trying to catch her breath.

'No, just dozing,' she said, her whole body still throbbing. 'Could you put the kettle on?'

'Sure,' he said, turning back towards the kitchen and buying her a few more seconds to recover.

Oh my goodness, that was close.

'How was your day?' she called out, a little too loud as he came back and stood beside her, leaning down to kiss her glistening forehead as the low whistle of the boiling water began to build.

'Interesting. James handed in his notice.'

'Oh?'

'Yeah, he's moving over to Integen,' he said, sitting down on the lounger next to hers. 'Tom's putting him on gardening leave.'

'When he's going?'

'Two weeks.'

'But that's before-'

'Yeah, I know,' he raised his eyebrows in dismay and then swung his legs up and lay back. 'You okay? You're sweating.'

'I'm fine, just a little warm.'

'How was your shift?'

'Good, I had a nice old man with a hip dislocation who was telling me all about his wife and his mistresses, that was *very* entertaining,' she laughed, taking a deep and uneven breath. 'And a pretty young girl who works on a cruise ship as a singer and she had a few interesting stories to tell. People are very *naughty* on cruise ships. She was telling me that there are whole cruises for *swingers.*'

'Oh, really?'

'*Mhm*, she worked on one for six months. She got quite used to turning down invitations from older couples to join them in their cabins.'

Chapter One

'*Oh*,' he said, smiling.

'Sounded quite exciting to me,' said Emilia. 'Other than that, it was quiet. Although the MRI scanner broke down, so that's going to create a backlog for a few days.'

'That's a shame,' said Cassian.

She watched as he leaned forward and drew off his tie before unbuttoning his shirt.

Handsome didn't cut it. Cassian was *hot*.

Emilia's heart rate fastened as a new idea formed in her mind. Her husband's physique was *toned*, to put it mildly. He ran ten kilometres four times a week, lifted weights, and cycled to work most days at a shared office in the city centre, and during lunch, he went to the gym.

Her sister Alice referred to Cassian as *The Greek*, and Emilia had often wondered if his past hid some middle-eastern ancestry with his olive skin and his thick dark hair. For a whole summer a few years ago she had buried herself in discovering their shared family histories, but she had hit a roadblock around one hundred and fifty years ago on his side and had eventually lost interest, telling herself she would pick it up again one day.

She couldn't help herself around him though, and ever since they'd met, all those years ago, they had been unable to keep their hands off each other, and although she naturally worried that one day their mutual attraction might falter, she didn't see it happening any time soon.

Fantasies about fictional men and swinging cruise ships aside. Besides, right now she was feeling horny, courageous and very, *very* kinky, and Josie had gone rather quiet next door.

She stood up quietly, letting her skirt settle down around her thighs, and smiling as her knickers dropped down onto the decking between her feet, and then she tip-toed softly across the warm wooden slats of the decking, letting the strap of her top fall off her shoulder to her elbow and exposing her breast.

Quickly and quietly she stepped over her husband and lowered herself down, straddling his legs and unfastening his belt, and before he knew what was happening, she was pulling his trousers down and sliding up and over him.

'Em, *what are you-*' he managed to say before she placed a finger over his lips as his eyes widened, and then as she knelt up she felt him *surge* and *grow* beneath her, teasing her, then she slipped down onto him and *sighed*.

*

The two of them had showered together after making love in the garden, drying each other off, and kissing and cuddling intimately as they'd made their way into their bedroom, and now, half an hour *post-garden sex* Emilia was laid out flat on their bed, her silk gown draped beneath her as a gentle breeze from the open window teased out goose-pimples across her skin.

Her toes curled as Cassian's hands slid down her spine and kneaded the skin above her bottom, pressing his fingers deep into the small of her back as she elicited a gentle moan.

As she lay there, lost in his touch, she found herself thinking back to just before he'd come home, and how she'd lost herself when she'd pictured him in her fantasy. The four of them together, being watched as she was taken by the Duke, kissing Elizabeth's lips and caressing her naked bosom, and to her surprise, she felt herself getting aroused again as her imagination ran away from her.

Was this something she wanted? No, it was *too* naughty. Wasn't it?

Cassian leaned down and began to kiss the nape of her neck, the bristles of his short beard prickling her skin and sending shivers down to her belly button, and she felt a brief surge of audacity. She *desperately* wanted to tell him about her fantasy, to share it with him and explore it together, but it seemed too taboo, even for them. Their marriage was built on communication and honesty, and she hated keeping anything from him, but she was worried that this might be going too far.

'So that was, unexpected?' he said, breaking the silence as he kneaded her shoulder blade.

'I liked it,' said Emilia, smiling into the duvet. 'Did you?'

'*Yes*,' he laughed. 'You certainly did. Did you… *you know?* Twice?'

She nodded and smiled, grinning with satisfaction. For a while, they were quiet again as he massaged her back and shoulders, but Emilia's mind was racing.

Making love to her husband in the garden had been even more exhilarating than touching herself. They hadn't been particularly quiet about it either. But it wasn't just the thought of being caught that turned her on, it was the thought of someone watching them as they were being intimate. Had Josie stopped what she'd been doing, and peeped through the fence?

'Cass, is there anything else you want to do? In the bedroom?' she asked, suddenly. The words came tumbling out of her mouth before she'd thought about them, and she felt flushed with a sudden sense of apprehension as her tongue got the better of her.

'Sunday afternoon blow jobs,' he said immediately.

She laughed, relaxing a little, 'I'm *serious*,' she said, going with it. 'Is there anything you want to do, that we don't already do?'

'Other than surprise garden sex?'

He continued to caress her shoulders, working his way slowly down her spine. 'Maybe more dirty talk?' he said.

'Like, *fuck me harder* or *suck my dick, you little slut?*' she laughed, blushing as she spoke.

'Somewhere between the two. More like, talking about fantasies. Why? Where is this going?'

'I'm just curious,' she said.

'What would *you* like?' he asked.

'I don't know,' she said, then she paused, feeling nervous and ashamed but desperate to tell him. 'There is something.'

He stopped kneading her back. 'What is it?'

'I'm scared to say,' she said. Scared didn't cut it, she was petrified, but she'd started this.

'Tell me, you can trust me.'

She lay still, frozen and ridged and a little panic-stricken. How was she supposed to bring this up? How did other people do it? *Hey, honey. I kind of want to see what it might be like to get fucked by another couple? You down?*

Instead, she said, 'Have you ever cheated on me?' and immediately regretted it.

'Twice this week,' said Cassian. 'Once with your sister.'

Emilia went to roll over, but her husband's strong hands pinned her back down and she felt his lips at her ear.

'Not once, and not ever,' he said, his voice barely a whisper, sending tingles across her scalp. 'I am yours and you are mine.'

'*You suck*,' she said as he let go and continued to caress her. 'Haven't you ever thought about it though?'

'No, have you?' he said.

'No.'

He continued to move his hands down her body towards her ass, his favourite play zone.

'What about checking out other girls?' she said.

'Is this what we're gonna do tonight? We're gonna fight?' he laughed.

'*No*,' she said, starting to feel annoyed. 'Stop teasing, we've been together since *school*. I'm the only girl you've *ever* slept with. You've *never* once thought about fucking another woman?' Cassian hesitated and Emilia grinned. 'You have, haven't you?'

'There's a *huge* difference between attraction and acting on attraction,' he said carefully, navigating the minefield that he'd unknowingly stumbled into. 'I have seen and met other women and thought they were attractive, but I haven't asked them for their number. What's this about?'

'What if we're missing something?'

'Like Sunday afternoon blowjobs?'

'*Shush*. What if I'm *not* the best sex you'll ever have? What if there's some *other* girl out there that would fuck your brains out and leave you begging for more?'

'I'm literally on top of you right now, naked, hard and thinking about how to get you in the mood for round two. What more do you want, Em?'

'So why did your mind go straight to *Alice* when I asked?' she said, feeling defensive now.

'Because you asked a stupid question, so you got a stupid answer.'

'*That's not fair*,' she said, this wasn't going how she'd wanted this conversation to go.

Cassian stayed silent, moving his hands back up to her shoulders. After a while, he spoke again, carefully. 'Do you *want* to sleep with other people?' he said.

'Do *you* want to?' said Emilia.

'No, you answer my question. I already answered yours,' he said.

She stayed quiet, then shifted her weight and reached behind her, blindly searching until she found her husband's cock and then she began to gently roll it between her thumb and forefinger. '*Maybe*,' she said in a whisper.

He twitched in her grasp. Slowly, he tightened his grip on

her shoulders and *squeezed* as he rocked his hips back and forth against her ass. 'Do you have someone in mind?' he said, curious but with a hint of pain in his voice.

She shook her head from side to side quickly. 'No, I don't mean like that.'

He was clearly confused now, somewhere between feeling jealous and upset, and surprisingly, incredibly turned on. 'Would you like to be fucked by another *man?*' he said. Emilia felt his cock harden as he spoke.

She said nothing, petrified of answering. Then quietly, barely more than a whisper. 'Yes. But not without you there.'

Immediately she felt a flood of emotions rush through her body, as though her whole being was tingling and surging, almost like panic, her nervous system dumping a dose of adrenaline into her chest, stomach and face. Slowly she wrapped her fingers one at a time around his cock and began to slide up and down, then she slid her legs apart just an inch. In response, Cassian ran his fingers along her inner thigh, slowly teasing his way up, then she buried her face in the pillow and let out a slow moan as he brushed against her wet lips.

She couldn't *believe* what she had just said, but it felt liberating to say it.

His finger circled her clit from behind and she felt a powerful tingle inside her body.

Cassian leaned forward and moved his body in line with hers, and then he whispered into her ear. 'I'd like to watch you get fucked by another man,' and then he slid his cock deep inside her.

Oh. Yes.

Emilia's whole body tensed in surprise as a powerful feeling began to build up from deep within her. It was like an eruption, as though a dam had burst at his words, rushing and gushing and flooding and overcoming her, and in that

Chapter One

moment of sheer ecstasy, feeling him penetrate her, she shuddered and *came*, squeezing him tightly with her pussy, and then a second later he slid back out of her again, giving her a moment to recover.

Feeling utterly ashamed he buried her face in the pillow, embarrassed by what she had said, and by how quickly she had orgasmed. After a while, her breathing returned to normal, and she plucked up the courage to roll over and look at him.

His eyes were closed and he was smiling, so she leaned in and kissed his lips. 'I'm sorry,' she said. 'I got carried away.'

'Don't be sorry,' said Cassian, opening his eyes. 'I enjoyed it, it's nice to hear what turns you on.'

'It… doesn't just turn me on though,' she said slowly.

Cassian stroked her hair and ran his fingers down her cheek, then he frowned. 'What do you mean?'

'It's not just a heat of the moment thing,' she said. 'I've been thinking about this a lot.'

'Okay,' said Cassian, nodding. She could feel him tensing up.

'I love you,' she said quickly. 'And it's not that you're not enough. It's not that *at all*. You're *more* than enough,' she paused, trying to think of an analogy. 'It's like having too much food on my plate. I want to share you - *share us* - with someone else.'

Emilia felt like she was finally piecing a puzzle together in her mind and she continued quickly as Cassian kissed her forehead.

'I want to share *all* of this,' she said. 'It's so wonderful what we have, I can't explain it any other way. I'm not even sure that it's possible to articulate. It's like a *feeling*, a throbbing sensation in my chest, and I want to burst when I think about it. I want to *share* and be *shared*.'

'That sounds good,' he said.

'*Really?*' she sat up in bed, her breasts distracting Cassian's eye, making him smile.

'Yes, it makes sense,' he said. 'But we've *never* been with anyone else before, just each other. If we do this, and we find someone to explore this with, there's no going back. We can't *undo* it. I don't want to lose you.'

'That's just it, you *won't* lose me. Even if I'm watching you fuck another woman and suddenly I'm overwhelmed with jealously, I will forgive you and I will forgive myself.'

'I don't think you can say that,' he said as he kissed her again. 'Perhaps you would, maybe you wouldn't. Either way, we shouldn't rush this. If it's *really* what you want then we should talk about it when we're not in bed together. When there's no expectation of sex.'

'Is this actually something you *want* though? If it isn't, then we won't talk about it again,' she said, serious all of sudden. She held his hand down as he tried to stroke her face.

'I need some time to think about it,' he said after a moment's hesitation. 'To process the idea.'

Then he grabbed her cheeks and started kissing her face, her nose, her ears, her hair and her lips as she giggled, and before long, they were making love again.

*

Emilia's eyes fluttered open as her dreams faded, but for a few blissful moments, she clung to them, the warmth of soft skin fading, the touch of someone's fingers… she sighed and took a breath, then her heart filled with guilt and she rolled over, only to find that Cassian was gone.

For what felt like a few seconds, her heart stopped. *Had he left?* And then the sweet smell of freshly baked croissants and coffee swarmed her senses and she relaxed, listening as her husband's familiar footsteps ascended the stairs.

Chapter One

'Oh my goodness,' she said, rubbing her eyes as he pushed open the door with his foot. 'This smells amazing.'

He leaned forward as he approached and kissed her on the forehead and a moment later she stretched and sat up, anxiety falling off her like a waterfall.

'Oh gosh, hang on I need a wee,' she laughed, pushing the covers aside suddenly but being careful not to knock over the coffee. Standing up, naked and barefoot from the night before, she rushed into the en-suite, swinging the door closed behind her with a cheeky grin.

'Did you mean what you said last night?' she said, calling out from behind the closed door.

'What did I say last night?' said Cassian, a tone of cheekiness evident in his voice.

'*Don't*,' she laughed. 'You *know* what I'm talking about.'

But he didn't reply and a moment later, Emilia nipped out of the little room her chest thumping as she walked back to the side of the bed, feeling vulnerable again.

'Yes, I meant it,' he said, looking down. 'But I did say I needed more time to think about it.'

'Wouldn't you be jealous though?'

He hesitated, glancing up into her eyes. 'Yes, in a way, but I trust you, and I love you, and that wouldn't change.'

She sat down on the bed again and picked up her coffee, cradling the warmth in her palms. 'I love you too,' she said, tucking her knees up beside her. 'But this could really change us, I don't want to lose you. We are literally talking about another man putting his cock inside me, fucking me, coming inside me, making me come.'

Her husband's face flushed and he recoiled slightly, rocking back on the bed. 'This is a bit of a heavy conversation for breakfast in bed, but yes, *I know*. And maybe me doing the same to another woman. How does that make *you* feel?'

'*Nervous*,' she said. 'But also, really excited. I think that's what I'd like, another couple,' she nabbed a croissant from his plate, and bit a small piece off.

'That's how I feel too,' he laughed. He reached out a moment later and put his arms around her and pulled her close to him.

'You're hard,' she giggled.

'Of course I am,' he grinned.

She licked her lips and wrapped her arms around his neck as he continued. 'Look, I'm not going to know how I'll feel until we do it. But I do know it won't change how I feel about *you*,' he said. 'I *know* I'll still love you.'

'Will you though?'

'Yes.'

'Are we really going to do it then?'

Cassian nodded and rolled his eyes, grinning madly. '*If you want to.* You never have to do anything you're uncomfortable with.'

'I want to try,' said Emilia earnestly. She put her hand on his cheek and kissed him deeply, her tongue brushing against his. Then she pulled back suddenly, gasping, a look of shock on her face.

'What about kissing? Can we *kiss* them?'

'Yes, we can kiss them,' he said laughing.

'Oh good, I like kissing.'

'We should set some boundaries though,' he said, looking serious again.

'Like what?' said Emilia.

'Like, anything you're not comfortable with doing.'

She nodded. 'I thought about this, and I don't know if there is much I'm *not* comfortable with. I mean aside from violence and choking.'

'Well then that's a boundary,' he said. 'If we meet someone who's into that, we make it clear that that's a hard *no*. Then they can take us or leave us.'

Chapter One

'Okay, yeah. So no violence, slapping, choking, nothing forced. I don't like that. And no cheating, I don't want a three-way with someone's husband or wife.'

Cassian nodded. 'Boundary number two.'

'Maybe they could be a *little* rough though,' she smiled, going slightly red in the cheeks. He laughed and smiled as she continued. 'I want you to understand why I want this though. This isn't like, a way to cheat and get away with it. I don't want to just steamroll you into letting me fuck another guy. And it's not because we've only ever been with each other, although that is *kind of* a part of it.'

'You want to share what we have,' he said.

'Yes, but it's more than that. I do want to share what we have, but also I want us to share in *another* couple's love. It's not just about us, it's about them too. Think about how much trust it will take for us to do this, and then remember that they will be taking that leap as well. I don't want us to just go out and fuck a couple of swingers, it might be fun - don't get me wrong - but that's just *sex*. Maybe we should do that first, but this is about making a connection. Maybe to find that connection we'll have to shag a few strangers, but I want to feel loved and safe and warm.'

Cassian smiled as his wife continued.

'And I want to know what other people do,' she said, a little more shy than usual. 'I mean what we have is amazing, but wouldn't it be fun to *feel* what other people feel? And to *feel* it with them? Knowing what it's like? I'm sorry I'm rambling.'

'I want this too. You brought this up, but it's something I've thought about before.'

'It is?' said Emilia.

He nodded. 'It's crossed my mind what it would've been like to sleep with other girls. If they'd have felt different, looked different, *smelled* different, all that kind of thing. And there are girls I've looked at and thought, *damn, that would be fun if I wasn't in love*. But it always comes back to *you*. You make me happy, and you can't get better than that. So if you're saying that you think this will make us even happier than we are now and that we can share our love with others? Then it can't hurt to try because we *can't* go down from *here*,' he held his hand up as high as it would go.

'You don't just want to fuck another hottie?'

'Yes, I want to fuck a *hottie*,' he laughed. 'But being *hot* isn't the only reason I'd want to do her.'

Emilia wrapped her arms around him suddenly, holding him tight and pressing her cheek against his chest, then just as quickly she leaned back. 'I have a *book* I want you to read,' she said.

He smiled and enveloped his arms around her as he kissed the top of her head, breathing deeply through his nose, practically inhaling her.

'I love you,' he said after a while.

'I love you, too.'

*

Emilia sat comfortably, waiting impatiently for her sister in her favourite little cafe, nestled amongst the trees of the local park, and situated just a short walk from their home.

Spring was underway and she sat gazing out of the window at the blossom tree that overhung the entrance, the beautiful pinks and whites of the petals shimmering in the evening sun.

She had texted Alice that afternoon, once her shift had finished, and asked to meet up so they could talk. Her sister had agreed immediately and said she was working late, but that she would be happy to take time off from work for half an hour to chat whatever it was over, but also because

Chapter One

Alice *loved* a good bit of gossip.

She sipped at her coffee. It was uncomfortably warm still, but she'd been nursing it for ten minutes now and it hadn't reached drinkable temperature yet. She'd asked them to make it inside her reusable cup, but the insulation was so good it seemed to disregard the laws of physics and heat up after the drink was poured in.

She was nervous, and not just because her neighbour had been acting weird when she'd left the house this morning, making Emilia wonder if she had seen or heard them making love the previous day. She was nervous mostly because Alice was late, but also because of what she wanted to talk to her about.

She must have been delayed at work, thought Emilia, but it always worried her when friends or family were not on time. She was naturally anxious and found it hard to stop her imagination from running away with dark thoughts about what fate might have befallen whoever it was she was meeting with.

She snapped herself out of the mental picture of Alice being hit by a bus, as her very much alive sister walked in through the entrance, and she waved, watching as her tall, gorgeous and leggy blonde sibling headed over swiftly, turning the heads of several patrons as she approached.

'Hey gorgeous,' she said. 'How're things?'

Emilia got up and hugged her tight. 'I'm good,' she said.

'Did you order me anything yet?'

Emilia shook her head and sat back down as Alice darted off again returning a few minutes later with a mug full of steaming mocha.

'I'm sorry,' she said, looking genuine. 'I know you hate it when I'm late, but I was stuck in a meeting with Tony and Giles and you know how they have to explain everything back to each other three times. *Skip to the fucking end guys*. I swear you could boil most of the meetings I have down to two sentences, *we want the thing, but we want it cheaper.*'

She sipped at her coffee, and Emilia did the same, now it had finally dropped to an acceptable temperature.

'So what's going on?' she said, smiling brightly.

Alice was two years older than Emilia, and much more liberal. For a start, she hadn't married the first boyfriend she'd ever had. She had *never* married, in fact, and didn't seem to be planning to do so anytime soon. She was openly bi-sexual too, which had rather surprised their parents the first time she'd bought a girl home from college. Dad had decided it was just a sleepover, but they all had ears and knew what was really going on.

Alice was also *whip-smart* and a brilliant mathematician. She had graduated from Oxford University with a first and landed a job as a corporate accountant for an international law firm that included several governments amongst their high profile clients, but the job had also meant that she could stay living in Oxford where they had been brought up and be close to her sister and their parents. Although she often had to travel, her base was always back home. They both took comfort in knowing they were usually never more than half an hour apart.

Emilia looked around nervously and then leaned in closer.

'Oh shit,' said Alice, sitting up. 'Is this serious?'

Emilia laughed and shook her head.

'What is it then?'

'Cass and I,' said Emilia. 'Um, I don't know how to say this.'

'*You're breaking up?*' said Alice, a look of shock crossing her face.

'*No, no!* Nothing like that,' she said, waving her hands and smiling as her sister's shoulders relaxed. 'Okay, so you know how you are, like... free?'

Chapter One

'Like, free?' she said in air quotes. 'As in, I'm not locked up in the local supermax? Or I'm a cheap shag?'

Emilia laughed again, she loved sparring with her sister. 'You should be locked up and you are definitely *not* a cheap shag,' she said. 'No. I mean, how you are free to, you know… have, relations? With, whoever you want.'

'Yes?' said Alice, her face contorting in confusion.

'Well, Cass and I have been talking-'

'I'm not having an incestuous threesome with you,' she interjected. 'I mean don't get me wrong, I'd fuck *Cass*, but I'm not fucking *you*.'

'Stop interrupting,' said Emilia, laughing hard. 'And you two *really* need to shag and get it out of your system.'

Alice snorted this time, drawing the attention of a nearby elderly couple who smiled kindly in their direction. She grinned back, winked and took a small gulp of her drink, still laughing.

'*Shush*,' said Emilia, waving her hands to quiet her down. 'Listen. Cass and I have been talking… about, *opening up* our relationship.'

Alice's eyes flew wide open and she leaned forward almost spitting out hot coffee. As she tried to gulp it down she burned her throat and dribbled some of the hot black liquid onto her hands.

'Holy shit, *Em*. I always figured that one day you two would finally discover a *kink*, but you're gonna do a *marathon* before you even tried running? Maybe let him stick his dick in your ass first, before you let him fuck other women.'

Emilia smiled at Alice and raised her eyebrows.

'*Oh my god*, you've already let him stick it up your bum? I don't even know you anymore. When did you become edgy?'

'Stop it,' said Emilia, blushing.

'So what's made you want to do this? Are you guys still

happy together?'

'Yes, absolutely. That's a large part of it. It may sound weird, but we're completely and utterly comfortable with each other. We're happy, we're in love, and we trust each other intimately.'

'Until you fall for someone else.'

'That won't happen.'

'Why not?'

'Because I love Cass,' she said. 'And because even if I did start to like someone else, I would still love Cass.'

'You fall in love fast, Em. You fell in love with your first boyfriend, and then you fucking married him.'

'That's a bad example because it's the *only* example. I love him, and you know I do.'

Alice stared at her sister, probing her. Then she smiled. 'Test passed. I think,' she said. 'Just don't be saying this out loud and inside you're thinking that you want to do this to save your relationship, or because you think he wants to, or because you just want to fuck around.'

Emilia shook her head.

Alice looked around at the other people in the cafe and then leaned in. 'Orgies are the fucking best.'

'Oh my goodness,' said Emilia. 'Seriously?'

She nodded, laughing. 'Hell yes,' she said. 'In fact, there's a masquerade ball in a week.'

'What's that?'

'Everyone dresses up in black-tie, lingerie and evening wear and you wear these old ornate masks, or quite frankly whatever you can find in the charity shop. You basically mask up and spend an evening mingling with other couples. There's usually a buffet, theatrics, some musical entertainment and then if you're interested, and stay on past the end of the night, they open up a bunch of private rooms and everyone gets naked and starts *fucking*.'

Chapter One

'Oh *gosh*,' said Emilia, leaning forward.

'It's not strictly just for swingers or whatever, it's like a high society thing, mingle with the big wigs, push your business card around, network, and later if you're up to it, fuck someone else's husband or wife.'

She raised her eyebrows at her sister, invitingly.

'Maybe,' said Emilia.

'If you want I can get you both tickets? It's not exactly the sort of thing you can pick up online.'

'I should probably talk to Cass first,' she replied, but she was already getting excited.

'I'll get you the tickets, there's no pressure. You don't have to stay, just go and have a good time on me and see where the night goes.'

'Cass was talking about *boundaries* the other night?'

'Have you set some?'

'No, well, sort of,' she said, concerned that she'd done something wrong.

'Probably for the best, if you want to really enjoy yourself. But if you do set boundaries, stick to them. Make them a golden rule, never to be broken and then *don't* break them. Once the trust goes, it all falls apart. I've been there, and it's shit.'

'Thank you, I knew I could talk to you about this,' said Emilia. 'Wait, will you be there?'

Alice shrugged, 'Maybe?' she said. 'Perhaps Cass and I could *finally* get it out of our system, eh?'

'I'd let you,' said Emilia, without hesitation.

Alice's eyes widened again. '*Wow*, and on that sex-bombshell, I'd better go back to work,' she stood up and downed the rest of her Mocha and then hugged her sister tight, kissing her on the cheek and then holding her shoulders. 'You ever need to talk about this, don't hesitate. Nothing is taboo between us, okay? I love you.'

'I love you, too. Thank you.'

She winked and turned to leave and then spoke loudly. 'Even if it's about *bum stuff*,' and with that, she walked out the door of the cafe, to silence, save for the tinkle of crockery as Emilia went bright red and sat straight down, desperately trying to shrink into her seat but failing miserably.

*

Alice delivered the tickets in person a few days later and Emilia had excitedly opened the door to greet her.

'I haven't asked Cass yet,' she whispered conspiratorially, as her sister stepped over the threshold. 'Do you think I should surprise him?'

'Surprise him? With an orgy?' said Alice. 'Maybe one step at a time, Em.'

'Oh, okay. Are you coming in?'

'No, I have to dash. I've got to meet with a client. In fact, I'm going to be away for a few days in Germany.'

'That's not too far,' said Emilia, relaxing a little. She always became anxious when her sister travelled.

'No, thankfully. Had to pull two all-nighters this week, although a long plane journey would've been nice to reset the clock.'

'When are you back?'

'Saturday, just in time for the ball.'

'So you're going?' she said, hopeful.

'Maybe,' said Alice. 'It all depends on how knackered I am when I get back.'

'Let me know if you're up to it,' said Emilia.

'I will not,' she winked and shushed her fingers to her lips. 'I've got to go, take it easy, Em and don't rush things.'

Emilia closed the door as Alice drove away, then she walked back into the living room where Cassian was

Chapter One

watching morning television.

'Who was that?' he asked, looking up as he turned down the volume.

'Alice, she popped by to give us some tickets for an event next weekend.'

'She's not coming in?' he said, looking past her into the corridor.

'Don't be too disappointed,' she sighed with a wry grin. 'She's off to Germany.'

Her husband nodded and turned back to the TV. 'What's the event?' he asked.

Emilia sat down on the couch and opened the envelope. 'It's a masquerade ball? She might not make it, but she's given us some tickets.'

'Like, tuxedo and a mask? How decadent.'

'There's an after-party too.'

'Oh yeah?'

Emilia nodded, but Cassian's attention was back on the television now, watching and listening to the pretty blonde news reporter reading out the headlines of the day.

'Where everyone gets naked and fucks,' she said quietly.

Cassian turned back to her, brow furrowed. 'What?'

Emilia smiled, blushing. 'There's an after-party, we don't have to go though, but Alice says it's a lot of fun.'

'Wait, you spoke to *Alice* about this?'

Emilia nodded. 'We talk about everything.'

Cassian continued to stare, wide-eyed. 'And she's okay with it?'

'*Yes*. Come on, this is Alice we're talking about. If you're not sure about going, that's fine.'

She got up and walked off into the kitchen as Cassian called after her and then followed.

'I'm sorry, I'm just a bit surprised,' he said, placing his bowl of cereal down on the side. 'This is going a bit quicker than I thought it would. The other day we were talking about opening up our marriage and now we've got tickets to an *orgy* at the weekend and your sister knows all about it? It's a lot to take in.'

Emilia stayed quiet, looking down at the floor, her hand resting on the kitchen counter surface as Cassian picked up the tickets and looked them over.

'The Carnaval de Débauche?' he said, raising his eyebrows. 'So… what happens at the after-party?'

'I don't know. Alice says that it's just for whoever wants to stay on.'

'There must be more to it than that.'

Emilia shrugged. 'Maybe they give out secret invites while we're there?'

'Your name's not on the list, because you're not *hot* enough?' he joked.

Emilia shrugged. She was beginning to feel a bit deflated.

'What about cameras?' said Cassian, looking up as he fingered the embossed card. 'I don't want to end up in the local paper, I think the boss might have a few words to say about it.'

'There's no way they'd let cameras in, but I don't really know.'

He put the tickets back down on the side and then looked over at his wife. 'I know, I'm sorry,' he said. 'It's just *huge*. Maybe, could we go to the ball and if we're not feeling comfortable, we just leave at closing time?'

Emilia looked back up at him and smiled. 'Yeah that's fine,' she said. 'I'm sorry, I don't want to make you uncomfortable. I'm just excited about this.'

She stepped forward into his arms and they hugged.

'Don't be sorry, let's just go, and see what happens,' he said with a smile.

Emilia looked up at him, with her big eyes full of hope.

Chapter One

'Are you sure?'
 'Let's do it.'

*

CHAPTER TWO

The Carnaval de Débauche was taking place at a secret mansion somewhere on the outskirts of Oxford and after signing up and verifying their identities - a stage which had nearly put Emilia off entirely - she had been informed that she would receive a text message an hour beforehand letting them know the location of the event.

Now they were following a Jaguar down a long, illuminated, tree-lined driveway which led to a secluded mansion with enough parking for several hundred guests.

The property itself was bathed in yellow light, lit by spotlights from below, and the ground floor was punctuated by two-storey high Victorian windows, each one almost twenty-foot tall, with thick velvet curtains closed to the outside world.

As Cassian pulled up, under the supervision of a luminous parking attendant, he saw that the grounds were being patrolled by security, each one dressed in suits with earpieces and matching haircuts. This was clearly a well-organised event, he thought to himself as he stepped out of their battered Fiesta, and we are a little bit out of our depth.

He went around to Emilia's door and opened it for her, holding out his hand to help her step out. She looked *radiant*. Dressed in a deep purple, ankle-length evening dress, embroidered with gold stitching and a revealing neckline which Cassian found himself staring down, knowing he wouldn't be the only one this evening to enjoy the same view.

Or perhaps, *even more?*

The sudden, almost *intrusive* thought brought back that feeling of jealously again, maybe even possessiveness and he stifled it and took a deep breath.

He had watched her get dressed, and he had seen the pink and black lace knickers she had chosen, the thigh high stockings with the little bow that she had pulled on and clipped to the pink and flowery basque that made her breasts look like they were *overflowing*. She looked so stunning and heartbreakingly beautiful, that he didn't want her to ever leave the house again.

He focused his mind on how much he loved her. Telling himself that he wanted this too and reminding himself how much he wanted her to be happy. But his heart still ached at the idea of another man touching her and he had to swallow his pride and think about something else entirely to stop his legs from turning around, getting back in the car and driving away from all of this.

'I feel like a small fish in a big fucking pond,' he said quietly as she stood next to him, marvelling at the sight of the mansion.

'Does it matter?' she asked. 'We're here now. Shall we?'

She extended out her hand to him a moment later, and he took it and led her off towards the entrance. As they walked

Emilia adjusted her mask with her free hand. She had found an ornate and delicate lace disguise, with what appeared to be intricate craftsmanship, prickled with crystal and glitter. It was simple and stunning and moulded almost perfectly to her face, except for the eye holes which she was finding frustratingly small.

Cassian on the other hand had opted for a much more stark and bold choice. His was black and ivory with chessboard streaks and baroque embossing set against a cracked China backing. It covered two-thirds of his face, making him look like the Phantom of the Opera.

Emilia had laughed when he had first put it on, but she had to admit that he looked *devilishly* handsome and had told him so straight away. She was worried that she might end up being rather *left behind* this evening in the attention stakes.

As they approached the entrance, a small queue had formed, with two burly doormen verifying identities and performing searches of bags and coats. They had left their phones in the car, and Emilia felt a little vulnerable without them, but seeing that phones and cameras were amongst some of the items being confiscated and tagged, she felt a brief moment of relief.

Once inside the mansion, they were greeted by an exuberant and fancifully dressed man who directed them through to the ballroom, where the rest of the stunningly gorgeous guests were beginning to assemble and mingle.

It struck Emilia as she walked in, that she was somewhat overdressed, and that she wasn't quite young enough for the room. Most of the people in front of her were nubile twenty-somethings, clad in what was little more than lacy lingerie, and it was clear that they were all cut from the same cloth - toned, muscly, skinny and gorgeous - and at first, she found it quite intimidating. But it quickly became apparent that age was *not* a barrier, and she also realised that whilst the

Chapter Two

younger crowd had congregated together in large clumps, the older crowd was encircling the room in smaller, more cliquey pockets. Many of the groups were observing the younger ones. It felt a little uncomfortably like an auction of flesh, and it made her feel slightly uneasy.

Walking slowly, they carefully gravitated towards the outer edge of the room, away from the hustle in the middle before making their way hand in hand along to the buffet at the far end.

'Are you okay?' said Emilia. 'This is a bit weird, isn't it?'

'It's not quite what I was expecting,' laughed Cass. 'It feels a little bit like a school disco, but with masks.'

'Shall we get a drink? We don't have to stay if it gets too weird.'

Cassian nodded as they continued weaving their way through the crowd, squeezing their way past women dressed as though they'd walked straight off a porn set, some wearing little more than string, others more conservatively attired.

And then the lights went out.

Emilia grabbed for Cassian's hand in the dark.

There followed a low rumble, like thunder approaching, and then a voice reverberated around the room as a spotlight shone down from the ceiling, illuminating the entrance which was now flooded by a thick cloud of dry ice. Then the exuberant man appeared through the smoke.

'Welcome one, *welcome all.* Welcome ladies and welcome gentleman and welcome to all those in-between.'

There was a flash and a crash and then a series of bright lights flashed on and lit the space from innumerable angles, transforming what initially appeared to be a gaudy, baroque ballroom into a bright, colourful, sophisticated and almost theatrical space.

Hung above them in the centre of the room were three

giant masks, more than fifteen feet across, looking out and down, imposingly upon them all in every direction. There was more too. Somehow, whilst the original lights had been turned off and their attention had been drawn to the host, large Art Deco mirrors had been erected around the space, along with drapes that had unfurled from the ceiling. Venetian lamps and tables had sprung seemingly out of the floor, busts of Roman figures and Greek statues had appeared from nowhere, and when Emilia looked closely she realised that the statues were actually living performance artists, standing stock still and naked, covered in a dusty white powder that gave the appearance of stone.

It was unreal and her eyes were wide with amazement. After a few moments stood stock-still in awe she realised that she was still squeezing Cassian's hand and she slowly relaxed her grip. The atmosphere of the whole room had changed, it had gone from what seemed like a slightly awkward costume party, to, well… a *Carnival of Debauchery*.

The compere's theatrical voice boomed through the room again. 'And doth the evening hath begun, bare not your souls foul fiends of filth, but bare your flesh with masques of silk, on all fours though beggest sooth and in thine soul find ruin, and *truth*.'

With this, the room shuddered with the sound of drums and a thunderous bass line as the music began and in the centre, the younger crowd began to go wild.

Emilia was enthralled, but as much as she loved the intensity and theatrical power of it all, it was proving a little too much too soon so she tugged at Cassian's arm and pointed towards an anteroom off the main event, and they began to weave their way through the crowd together, hand in hand.

As they walked, a young woman, masked and dressed in an elegant and almost *entirely* see-through red-lace gown,

Chapter Two

slapped Cassian on the bum, pinching hard before disappearing into the crowd, leaving Emilia stood mouth agape in shock as her husband grinned and laughed.

Once they reached the side room, the sound of the music began to fade to a more manageable volume and they stepped over the threshold to find a more civilised scene, with couples talking, eating and drinking wine. Even the clothing that most of them were wearing was more in line with Cassian and Emilia's choices, and both of them began to relax a little, feeling more at home in this crowd.

'We should mingle,' she said, winking and then noticing her husband's expression. 'Are you okay?'

He nodded. 'Just a little intimidated.'

'I like your honesty,' she said, smiling. 'Come on, let's go find a nice group of people to slip into. We can be whoever we want, remember? We're in *disguise*.'

She pulled him forward with a squeeze of her hand, and then twirled and skipped away as she laughed, whilst Cassian drew a long deep breath, closed his eyes, and exhaled hard.

*

Cassian first saw Amy in the reflection of one of the eight-foot-tall baroque mirrors which had been erected around the room like monoliths. Her bright red hair had caught his eye, and he had found himself drawn back to look for her, tuning out of the droning conversation he was stuck in with an ageing banking executive from Slough.

'I just don't understand why they *insist* on increasing funding to support these initiatives,' the old man was saying when he was interrupted by a waitress offering a refill of his third drink of the evening.

Cassian took the opportunity to excuse himself and headed

towards the bathroom, leaving the complainer in the company of an equally disinterested woman, dressed in white with a mask that made her look a bit like a chicken.

As he feigned his exit, he looked across to where the attractive redhead was standing and found her again. Looking at her properly now, he saw that her mouth was ever so slightly asymmetric, her lip curling in one corner to form an alluring smirk.

She looked smart and driven, and he could see that she was holding the attention of the group that surrounded her and not purely because of her striking looks.

Then he saw that a tall man, with a sharp haircut and a well-fitted suit, wearing a mask which gave him the appearance of a crow, was leaning into her, his hand softly placed in the small of her back, pride clear in his expression as she spoke.

Cassian found himself drawn to her, like he had discovered the life of the party, or a flame in the darkness, so much so that he found he was staring, and then her eyes caught his, and for a brief and intense second they both gazed at each other, and she faltered.

He looked away, embarrassed, turning quickly and continuing on his way toward the toilets, unsure of what else to do. He wanted to look back, to catch her eye again and feel that connection, but he was too embarrassed to do so.

Inside the restroom, he headed into one of the cubicles and stood inside awkwardly before remembering why he was here, but as he relieved himself he kept replaying the look in the girl's eyes back in his mind.

She was *stunning*. He'd come here tonight with zero expectations and a feeling of *dread* in the pit of his stomach, worrying that his wife might want to enjoy this experience more than he did, but suddenly, in a single heartbeat, his foundations had been shook. Perhaps it was just the context

Chapter Two

of this party, this strange, wonderful and unusual event, or... could it be something more?

He closed his eyes and sighed, then he flushed, turned and opened the door and came out to see the red-haired woman's partner - the man in the crow mask - slowly washing his hands in the sink.

Cassian froze, and the man looked up, glancing at him in the mirror. 'My wife's quite the centre of attention, isn't she?' he said.

The man looked around and picked up a paper towel as Cassian slowly recovered, carefully stepping up to the sink to wash his own hands, whilst smiling politely and feeling somewhat nervous.

'My name's Mark,' said the man.

'Cassian', he replied as he grabbed a paper towel for himself and dried his fingers before taking the stranger's hand. 'She certainly draws a crowd.'

Mark laughed softly and turned back to the mirror. 'Are you married?'

'Six years,' said Cass. 'How about you?'

Mark nodded his head. 'Two,' he said. 'It's gone by in a flash.'

Cassian looked the man up and down in a flash as he glanced back toward the mirror. He was built, but not excessively - lean, powerful and rigid. His stature and poise were hard and his movements *snapped*. The haircut was the clue but the rest was the evidence.

'Are you military?'

Mark smiled. 'What gave it away?'

'You don't hide it well,' smirked Cassian.

'Ex. I work in protection now, mostly politicians, CEO's, a few rock stars. Charming people. Salt of the earth. How about you?'

'Is that how you met? You were her bodyguard?'

'No, it's almost as cliche though.'

Cassian laughed and turned as he began to make his way towards the door.

'Come and meet her,' said Mark. 'I already caught you staring at her, you may as well come and get a proper look.'

Cassian faltered as he reached the exit and realised he'd stopped walking.

'It's fine,' laughed Mark. 'She's gorgeous, it's hard not to stare. Come and say hello, she'd love to meet you.'

Mark gestured to the doorway, and Cassian, now more than a little flustered, pushed it open. The sound of the party rushed back and filled his senses once again, and on the other side of the door, he found a throng of people shouting and dancing.

'This way,' said Mark, touching Cassian's arm above the elbow to guide him. 'She won't have moved whilst she still has an audience.'

He followed on in a daze, squeezing and sliding his way through the party guests, smiling at various masked men and women. As he moved he was looking out for Emilia, hoping to catch her eye and beckon her over, and then he saw her near the bar. 'Wait, I'm just going to get my wife.'

Mark turned and nodded, 'Come on over to us when you're ready.'

Cassian met the man's eye for a brief moment, and then he turned and weaved his way quickly toward his wife, touching her lightly on the arm. She was in the middle of being accosted by a young lad of around twenty, who was excitedly telling her all about the latest developments in the world of robotics. 'Sorry to interrupt, Em, but we've got a date.'

'Oh?' she said, confused.

He leaned close and whispered in her ear. 'Follow me.'

Then he took her by the hand, much to the disappointment

Chapter Two

of the young lad, and led her through the throng of party-goers towards what Emilia could see was a stunningly beautiful red-haired girl, whose radiance seemed to effervesce upon those around her.

Emilia found herself experiencing a sensation she hadn't felt in years, perhaps not since school. She didn't know if it was the intensity of the party, or the thought of what may or may not happen later, or what Cassian had said about a *date*, but there was an unexpected spark of attraction towards this girl and she found herself desperately hoping that Cassian was taking her by the hand to meet *her*, and not someone else.

As the couple approached, the handsome and clean-cut gentleman to the woman's right turned and smiled and Emilia felt a sudden rush of excitement.

'Amy,' said Mark. 'There's someone I'd like you to meet. This is Cassian.'

Amy's jewel-green eyes met Cassian's and she smiled such a friendly and disarming smile that it seemed to make his embarrassment disappear into a gentle haze. She reached out her hand and he took it and softly shook.

'Cassian,' she said, stepping away from her audience with an apologetically demure glance.

As she spoke she reached out and touched his arm, and then she leaned in and whispered. 'I'm so sorry, I asked my husband to head off and find someone *normal* for us to talk to, I hope you don't mind?'

Cassian laughed. 'It's quite the peculiar event, isn't it?' he said, and at the same time, he brought Emilia forward, who was now feeling so shy she feared that *actual* butterflies might escape her mouth if she were to open it.

'This is my wife, Emilia.'

Amy reached out a hand to her and said. 'Well, you *are* stunning, no wonder you found yourself a handsome man like this.'

'Thank you,' she managed, grinning like a schoolgirl. She had to fight to stop herself from chewing her own hair.

'So what brings you two here then?' said Mark.

Emilia tried to keep herself from stuttering, but as Cassian began to speak, she managed to interrupt him and get a hold of herself. 'My sister gave us the tickets,' she said. 'She works for Berkshire Radcliffe, but they sent her out to Germany this week and she wasn't sure if she would make it back in time.'

'What does she do?'

'Corporate solicitor and accountant,' said Emilia. 'What do you guys do?'

'I'm a struggling artist, and muscles here thinks he's Kevin Costner.'

Emilia frowned and looked confused, but Cassian stepped in. 'Mark is a bodyguard.'

Her eyes widened. 'What sort of artist *are* you?'

'Oh *gosh*, sorry,' said Amy, her eyes widening as she grinned and touched her lips. 'He's not *my* bodyguard. Mark and I are married, but he *works* as a bodyguard.'

'Oh, I see,' said Emilia, embarrassed by her mistake.

'As for your question, I'm a *shit* artist, but Mark gets paid a silly amount of money, so I'm fortunate enough to spend my days exploring my creative side, although I'm starting to wonder if I have one. What about you two?'

'Marketing,' said Cassian.

'I'm a physiotherapist.'

'So how does a physiotherapist and a marketing guru meet?' she laughed.

'How does a bodyguard and an artist meet?' said Emilia, not quite ready to share their story of meeting at the tender age of fourteen.

'Touché,' said Amy. 'Fine, I'll go first,' she leaned in closer so she could talk a little more quietly. 'I was dating the lead singer of a rock band and Mark was leading his security detail. One night, Mr Rock Star got fucked up on cocaine and whiskey and beat the shit out of me. Mark stepped in, and I began questioning my life choices.'

'Oh my *goodness*,' said Emilia, stunned.

'I'm sorry to hear that,' said Cassian, taken aback.

'And apparently, my life choices led me *here*,' she swept her hand around the room and Emilia laughed.

'So how did *you* end up with an invite?' said Emilia, trying to divert the conversation.

'Through Mark's company, his security team is working the event and they had spare tickets. Although I'm pretending that I'm a world-famous but completely unheard of contemporary artist and that Mark is my elite bodyguard for the night. Mark, do the thing where you speak into your arm.'

Mark shook his head and laughed and then feigned looking serious, holding his wrist to his mouth. 'PPO-five to TFT, unauthorised members of the public in close proximity to priority one, request takedown. Over.'

Amy smiled and bit her lip. 'It turns me on more than I care to admit when he does that.'

Emilia let out a long slow breath in agreement, thankful for the mask which was hiding her blush. Amy reached out and touched her arm and laughed, then she took her hand and started pulling her towards the bar. 'Come on, I like you, let's go get some more drinks.'

As the girls disappeared into the crowd, Cassian turned to Mark. 'That wasn't as cliche as I was expecting, sounds like you did a good thing.'

'It worked out well for everyone, *Mr Rock Star* spent a little time in hospital, then a little time in jail, then a little time in rehab.'

'I'm no closer to figuring out who he was. That describes an awful lot of rock stars.'

Mark laughed, but clearly, he had no intention of revealing who his client had been.

A few minutes later the girls returned, with two more drinks each, holding out soft drinks for the men and keeping cocktails for themselves.

'So Emilia tells me you like to fuck her in the ass?' said Amy.

'What?' said Cassian, turning to Emilia shocked.

'What, I never said that?' said Emilia, equally surprised and embarrassed.

'But you *have*, haven't you?' laughed Amy. '*Oh my*, you guys are not as vanilla as I thought. You are *dirty*.'

Mark rolled his eyes, 'Sorry, two sips of Margherita and Amy loses all of her inhibitions.'

'What else do you like, Emilia?' she said, staring at her with her big probing, green eyes. 'Do you like it from behind? What's your favourite position?'

Emilia laughed, feeling emboldened by her mask. Amy was exciting. 'Reverse cowgirl and the jockey.'

'Oh my goodness, I love the jockey. Mark get's really deep when we do that like he's trying to *fuck* my cervix,' she burst into loud laughter and drank another gulp of her drink.

Mark was gently shaking his head, as Cassian looked on bemused.

Emilia leaned forward and loudly whispered. 'I love it when he fingers my ass,' which prompted Amy to almost spew Margherita in her face.

Cassian stepped forward now and put his arm around his wife. 'I think you're getting carried away,' he said, but Emilia shrugged him off.

'Oh come on, Cass, let your hair down,' she laughed.

'Yes, let's dance!' said Amy. Then she reached *past* Emilia, and to her surprise, grabbed *Cassian's* arm and pulled him into the crowd, boldly dancing with him to the thumping

Chapter Two

bass line.

Emilia watched them as Amy started grinding and sliding up against her husband and she suddenly felt a little left out. Seemingly sensing her disillusionment, Mark's hand appeared in front of her and beckoned an invitation to dance with him.

'Come on, it's best to meet her at her level after she's had a few,' he smiled. 'If you can't beat them, *join* them.'

Emilia took his hand with a blushing smile and followed him over to where Cassian and Amy were dancing, her husband looking *more* than a little intimated.

Now Amy turned her attention on Emilia, grabbing both her hands and twirling herself around, so her palms were on her hips, then she slid up and down and moved her new friend's wrists up and down her body, brushing past the edges of her breasts. Then she spun around and began pressing her ass into her crotch and holding her arms across her chest, all in time to the music.

She had *never* felt like this with a girl before, but Amy was something else, and to her surprise, she could feel herself getting more and more aroused. It was as though she was enchanting her, casting some sort of spell. If any other girl had danced like this with her before, she would have felt uncomfortable and walked away, but with Amy it was *thrilling*.

There was a hint of jealousy there too.

Amy and Cassian had some sort of connection that she didn't understand yet, and on one level she wasn't sure how she felt about it, and on another, it was *exhilarating*. Either way, she could feel herself starting to tingle with electricity.

As Amy spun around and into her again, Emilia buried her face into the girl's hair and breathed in deeply, and found it to be *intoxicating*.

The newly acquainted foursome danced for another half an

hour, before retiring to a nearby table for a further round of refreshments.

'This night is turning out far better than I thought it would,' said Amy, sitting down lightly on Emilia's lap. 'You guys are so much fun, and damn, you can dance, Em.'

Emilia, who by now was more than a little enamoured, and inebriated, started stroking Amy's thigh and nodding. 'I think we've had a great time too,' she said. 'Cass?'

'I'm exhausted,' said Cassian. 'So, probably, yes.'

'What time is it?' said Amy.

'Zero hundred hours,' said Mark.

'He means midnight,' said Amy, turning slightly and putting her arms around Emilia as she sat dangling her legs. 'And I think we'll need to be heading off. My carriage turns into a pumpkin if I don't leave before midnight.'

'But Cinderella?' said Emilia. 'Will I ever see you again?'

'Would you like to see me again?'

Emilia nodded.

'Give me your phone,' she said.

'It's in the car,' said Emilia.

'Oh shit, so's mine. Fuck. You'll just have to remember it then,' she said. 'We weren't even allowed to bring in a sodding pen. I know Mark looks like a badass, but he's not Liam fucking Neeson.'

'I could kill all three of you with a pen,' said Mark.

'Well, that's dark. Wait, do you have some lipstick?'

Emilia nodded and delved into her dress. '*And* I have pockets,' she said grinning. After rummaging around inside of them she produced a small red lipstick.

Amy turned to face her, smiling briefly as their eyes met for a moment too long, and then pushed the edge of the neckline of her dress to one side in order to write her number on the top of Emilia's left breast.

'Nice underwear,' she whispered as she drew close to her

Chapter Two

ear.

Emilia tried to control herself, but let out an involuntary shake and had to bite her lip as Amy wrote.

'*There*,' she said when she was done, practically tucking her new friend's boob back into her dress. 'Now, you have my number,' then she kissed Emilia on the cheek and sprung up into the air.

'Come on,' she said. 'Take me home and *spank me*, I think I've been a little naughty this evening.'

She winked, and then they were leaving.

Emilia watched with a mixture of jealously, disappointment and excitement as they left. There was a part of her that had wanted them to stay, and for them all to head to the after-party together, but for some reason, whilst Emilia fancied them both, the idea of heading off to a room together and shagging didn't feel like *enough* now.

'You okay?' said Cassian, moving closer as she pined.

Emilia turned to face him. 'I guess,' she said, nodding.

'Do you still want to stay?'

She looked around at the other guests, some of them starting to leave, others hanging back.

'Yes, I think so,' she said. 'We can stay for a bit maybe, and see what it's like?'

But something had changed inside of her, something was *different*. She didn't really understand what it was, but she felt strangely hollow as if she had found a key to a part of her soul that she didn't know existed, and then as suddenly as it had been opened, it had been *closed*, leaving her desperate for more.

She turned and tried to look for Amy and Mark, but they had already gone.

*
* * *

As the crowd thinned, Emilia and Cassian began to realise that a thinner stream of party guests were gravitating towards the central staircase that led up to the upper floors of the cavernous mansion, and as they began to head over, Emilia started to wonder who lived here. She guessed that they must be involved in the party somehow, or perhaps it was owned by a family who hired it out to functions like this, or maybe nobody lived here, and it was a corporate retreat of some kind. She also wondered just how many people did this sort of thing every week. If her own *sister* might be here, who else in her circle of friends was into this lifestyle?

At the foot of the roped-off staircase stood two men dressed in sharp and well-fitted dinner suits and wearing Venetian masks like all of the other men and women surrounding them. As each couple approached the stairs they were vetted and checked, before being allowed to ascend. She also noticed that only couples and single women were being allowed through. No single men were approaching the roped off concourse.

'Are you *sure* you want to do this?' asked Cassian, pulling her to a stop and squeezing her hand with a kind firmness.

She looked up at him, and then over toward the staircase, biting her lip and frowning, thinking back to the excitement of Amy and Mark. 'I don't know,' she said. 'But I don't want to regret *not* trying if we walk away now.'

Her husband nodded and then he pulled her in close to him, holding her against his chest and kissing her forehead with a warmth normally reserved for home.

As he pulled back, she looked up, staring deeply into his eyes. 'Do *you* want this?' she said.

He nodded slowly. 'One step at a time though.'

'One step at a time,' she repeated. Then she took his hand, squeezed it and led him slowly toward the stairs as her heart began to race.

Chapter Two

As they approached, one of the stern-looking men turned to greet them and Emilia noticed him appraising them quickly as they drew near. 'Good evening, Mr and Mrs Black,' he said.

Emilia's eyes widened with surprise. 'Do we know you?' she said.

The man shook his head. 'No, Mrs Black. We memorise the features of each of our guests before they arrive to ensure a *personal* welcome.'

The man reached down and unclipped the rope, moving it aside for them to pass through. 'Miss Alice Hunter sends her best wishes,' he said as they reached the first step.

Emilia stopped and looked up at Cassian who was laughing quietly. 'Do you think she's here?' she said.

'I *hope* so,' said Cassian.

'If she is, then I wouldn't mind if you both wanted to...' she trailed off, a powerful jolt of fear and excitement pulsing in her chest as she spoke, making her feel dizzy.

Cassian lips went dry and he licked them, frowning. 'Really?'

Emilia nodded her head and smiled. 'She's beautiful, and I know you'd be kind. I'd almost rather you were with *her* than a stranger.'

Cassian stopped on the stairs suddenly, then leaned down and kissed his wife with such passion and love that she swooned, her legs turning to jelly as he held her.

As he pulled away she felt dizzy. 'I love you,' he said before they continued up the stairs.

'You be careful who you go kissing with those lips tonight,' she laughed, still wobbling.

As they neared the top, they saw another couple heading into one of the side rooms, and, not knowing what else to do, they followed.

As they approached the doorway, which was partially

closed, they peered inside and listened. Beyond the threshold were three young couples. The ones who had just arrived were still dressed in evening wear, but the other two couples were a little more *relaxed*. The two women were sat together, almost naked, entwined in each other's arms and kissing passionately as their male partners looked on.

The new couple that had walked in were standing near the door watching the others, and as Emilia observed, the two kissing women stopped and turned to appraise the new arrivals, before nodding. It was as if they had *approved* this new pair joining in, and Emilia suddenly felt incredibly self-conscious. She found that she didn't *want* to go in, that she was too afraid of being rejected. But Cass was already opening the door and pulling her gently by the hand inside.

The fully dressed newcomers turned to look at them both and smiled. The woman was *beautiful*, and Emilia watched with surprise as this brunette beauty locked eyes with her whilst she slipped off her dress, letting it fall to the floor around her ankles, revealing a red lace baby doll and matching stockings stretched up to the tops of her thighs, but that was all. She wasn't wearing any knickers, and as Emilia's eyes took this in, she blanched.

Unable to take her eyes off the girl, she watched as she walked around to the other two girls, stroking their shoulders as she passed and then she straddled one of the two other men, biting his lower lip as she sat down on his lap.

Emilia's face was a picture of shock. These women had *all* the control here, and it was incredibly intimidating. Her relationship with Cass had always been equal. She wasn't in charge and neither was he. It felt overwhelming to see these women employ such audacity and confidence, but it was equally empowering and she admired them for it.

But it wasn't quite what she was expecting either, or hoping for. She wanted *slow*, she wanted *sensual*, she wanted

Chapter Two

warmth and love. This felt raw and powerful and controlling.

She turned back to Cassian and shook her head and started towards the door.

The couples inside paid no more attention as they left, Cassian pulling the door closed as they came back out onto the landing.

'What's wrong?' he said.

'I'm sorry, it was just a bit too much,' she said, close to tears. 'I don't want that. I want *this*, but not *that*.'

'Maybe we could try a different room?'

Emilia nodded and looked down the corridor. The first door they came to was ajar, and she peered inside to find three naked couples already fucking. One of the women was sucking the cock of one man as she was being fucked from behind by another. She closed the door quietly and kept walking, although she was surprised to find that she was now a little more turned on than she was before.

The next door opened onto a much tamer scene. Inside were another two couples, and they were kissing what Emilia assumed was their *own* partners, but it wasn't clear and whilst the women were no longer wearing evening wear, the room didn't feel quite as intense as the first.

One of the girls looked up and smiled as she walked inside, pulling Cassian after her, then the girl went back to kissing the masked man on the large sofa as Emilia looked around.

The room was as big as the ground floor of their *house*. It was lit by a mixture of dull red lamps and warm orange spotlights, and in the centre was an enormous four-poster bed that stretched up to the ceiling, surrounded on all sides by thin privacy drapes.

To her right were two large deep red leather sofas that faced each other, and in the middle was an ornate coffee table bordered with stitched leather and mounted on what looked like the legs of a Stag. In the middle of the table was a bowl filled to the brim with a variety of condoms and lube.

Emilia stifled a laugh.

The whole scene was utterly decadent and uncomfortably gaudy, but this room felt far more comfortable and better paced than the others and she didn't feel quite so self-conscious.

She took Cassian's hand and with a heady mixture of anxiety, power and arousal, she led him over to the sofa.

As she drew near, she took a closer look at the other couples. The girl nearest the bed was tall and thin, and no older than twenty or twenty-two and from her new vantage point she could see that whilst she was kissing her bearded partner, her hand was also wrapped around his erect cock which she was stroking slowly as she moved her hips back and forth.

She paled as she realised what she was looking at and turned away sharply to see that the *other* couple were less clothed than she'd appreciated from the doorway. This girl was more petite but the man was stacked like a bodybuilder, his shirt and jacket wide open and his chiselled chest bare and shaved.

As she reached the sofa, Emilia turned Cassian around and pushed him down with the palm of her hand and then hitched up her dress and straddled him, forcing herself to be confident. He held her waist in his strong arms as she bent down to kiss him, and she felt his cock growing between her thighs as she pressed herself down.

She felt intensely aroused now, but she couldn't shake the feeling of anxiety in the pit of her stomach and she felt like instead of trying to understand what was causing it, she was just powering through, determined to break the physical and emotional barrier she felt existed between their old selves and what she *wanted* them to become.

Chapter Two

She glanced sideways and noticed that the tall girl's hand was sliding up and down faster now, and the bearded man, who was breathing loudly and occasionally moaning, was looking over at them both, staring whilst licking his lips.

Then she felt a sensation behind her, and in the corner of her eye, she saw movement as the petite girl's hands began to slide up Cassian's thigh. Before she could say anything, the tall girl was standing up and pulling Emilia upright, then turning her around slowly to face the bed.

The girl's lips were suddenly next to her ear and she blushed and shivered. 'Would you like to touch my husband?' she whispered, making the hairs on the back of her neck stand on end.

It was all happening so fast.

Before she could process what was happening, the girl was tugging on the zip of Emilia's dress and sliding it down as the bearded man looked up at her, stroking his cock harder and faster, and then suddenly, she started to *panic*.

The anxiety in her stomach spread and took over her whole body, but it wasn't because of the situation, not entirely. It was something else. Something *far* more important to her. She didn't want *this* girl to smudge the number that Amy had written on her breast, and then just like that, everything felt wrong.

I don't want this, she thought. This was just sex and it wasn't *right*. Not for them. She wanted them to have something *more* than this. She wanted them to feel a real connection, and she'd felt that, or at least something *like* that, with Amy and Mark.

She looked to the side and saw that the petite girl was moving her hands up Cassian's chest and was leaning up to kiss him.

'*No*,' she said. The word came out of her mouth far more forcefully than she'd anticipated.

The girl behind her stopped, the dress zip half undone as Cassian turned to look at her, and at the same time, the petite girl stopped, looking disappointed.

'I'm sorry, I don't think I'm ready for this,' she said, feeling shy all of a sudden. She moved away, her dress falling down over her shoulders as the tall girl smiled kindly.

'That's okay,' she said. 'It's hard the first time. You can just watch us if you want?'

Emilia shook her head. 'No, thank you,' she said as Cassian stood up looking concerned, watching as she began to walk backwards away from them all.

She reached the door and almost ran into the corridor and a moment later Cassian's arm was around her shoulder, his hand doing up her zip as his arm wrapped around her. 'Are you okay?' he said.

'Yes,' she shook her head. 'But I don't want this though.'

'You *liked* them, didn't you?' he said. 'Amy and Mark?'

She smiled at him. He knew *exactly* what she was thinking - somehow he always did.

She nodded. 'I don't want it to be like this,' she said. 'Not with strangers.'

Cassian smiled. 'Let's get out of here,' he said, winking.

Emilia took his hand in hers, and for a brief and fleeting moment, she thought about how it felt to hold Amy's hand at the ball - how it felt soft and smooth, and electrifying, just like Cassian's.

'Let's go,' she said, and as she started down the stairs she understood what that feeling was now, the one she had felt before they headed up the stairs, and why it had felt new and exciting.

It was the start of a crush.

*
* * *

Chapter Two

Emilia spent the whole ride home smiling and buzzing with excitement. The first thing she had done when they'd got in the car, was ask Cassian to read the slightly smeared number off her breast and save it into her phone.

She had never met *anyone* like Amy, and Mark was so nice and friendly, and *manly*. She had been thinking about them all the way back - what they were doing, if they were home already, and if Amy was bent over their bed, being *spanked* by her handsome husband. By the time they got home, her knickers were soaked through and she was more aroused than she had been in *years*.

The after-party had been exhilarating, she had pushed her boundaries and in doing so she had discovered that this wasn't just about sex. It was about finding an emotional connection, something personal, and she wondered if she might have found that tonight.

Cassian unlocked the front door and pushed it wide, waving his arm theatrically for his wife to walk through. 'My lady,' he said.

She stepped over the threshold and dipped a brief curtsy in his' direction as he followed her through. 'Would you care to join me in the bedroom, kind stranger?' she said.

'Why certainly, Miss. It would be my pleasure.'

'Oh, I am confident the pleasure will be *all mine*,' she winked.

Cassian ran towards her and she screamed and started up the stairs. He kicked the front door shut and gave chase, running up behind her and through the open bedroom door where he leapt on top of her, pinning her down with his powerful arms.

She looked small beneath him, and so different in her mask. More like a stranger than his wife, and it was turning him on more than he cared to admit.

He kissed her, pinning her arms above her head as he did

so, and she *writhed* in response.

'Oh sir, please. Let me go, don't have your wicked way with me.'

He shook his head at her, laughing and let go of her arms, sitting back up on the bed.

Concerned and a little frustrated, Emilia propped herself up on her elbows beside him. 'What's wrong?'

He looked at her and shrugged. 'If this doesn't happen how you want it to, will *this* be enough?'

'How *we* want it to,' she corrected. 'I want *you* to want this.'

'I *do* want this,' he reached out and placed his hand on top of hers. 'But I need to know that if it never becomes a reality, that *this* is good enough.'

Her eyes grew wide as she looked at him with an incredulous gaze of love and kindness, and nodded her head slowly.

'Cass, every morning I wake up next to you and I look across, and I think to myself, *how did I get this lucky?*'

He smiled and squeezed her hand as she continued.

'It's like, my heart is full and it's full because of *you*, but... it's got room to grow. When people have children, they don't halve the love they have for their partner to accommodate their child, their heart *grows*, and it gets bigger and bigger the more you love. *That's* how I feel, I want my heart to grow so I can love more, but my heart is *already* full.'

Cassian looked down then nodded. 'You are really good at this,' he said, laughing.

Emilia raised her eyebrows and smiled. 'I know, right?'

'When we were in that room tonight, I wouldn't have stopped you.'

'I know,' said Emilia.

'And that little blonde girl? She was *hot*.'

'She was blonde? I couldn't see *anything* in there.'

Chapter Two

'The point is, I would've supported you,' said Cassian, looking down at her on the bed.

'But it wasn't what you wanted,' she said.

'No.'

'Like I was saying. *How did I get this lucky?*'

'But, on the landing, when you said about Amy and Mark?' he continued.

She turned her head to one side and frowned. 'I really liked them.'

'I liked them too.'

She felt a surge of exhilaration. 'I don't want to just have sex with strangers, I want more than that, I want what we have together, with others. I want a connection, not a quick fuck.'

'That's what I want too.'

'Love shouldn't be defined by sexual exclusivity,' said Emilia. 'I'm not yours, you're not mine, we are a partnership that's built on respect. And if everything we do isn't about love and sharing and giving, then we're doing it wrong.'

He nodded, then just as he was about to respond, she continued.

'Also, it's about having *really* good sex.'

He smirked. 'I'm trying to be serious here.'

'So am I. I don't think you can have really, *really* good sex without a connection,' she smiled. 'Can I be honest with you?'

'Of course.'

'I *really* liked them.'

'Me too,' said Cassian. 'Amy seemed really fun, and Mark was a good guy.'

'So you'd be okay with them?'

'They seemed really nice.'

'You'd be okay with Mark, the bodyguard, poking me in the cervix?'

Cassian laughed and turned away. Then suddenly he whipped back around and gripped hold of her wrists, rolled her onto her front and pinned her back down on the bed. With his free hand, he flipped her dress up and over her back as she laughed, and looked down at her pink and black lace knickers. She squirmed in his grip, trying to turn her head to look back at him as his eyes followed the contour of her thighs, past the hooks that secured her stockings to the pink flowery basque that he'd coveted all night long.

Then, still holding her down with a single hand, he unclipped both of them and slid her whole body down until she was bent over the edge of the bed, knees on the floor. With his free hand, he quickly pulled down her knickers and let them fall to the floor around her legs, then she gasped as he approached her ear. She could feel his hot breath on the back of her neck as he spoke, sending goosebumps down her spine.

'You want to know if I'd be okay with him *fucking* you?' he said.

Emilia's mind *raced* with thoughts. He had never been this in charge before, and it was turning her on intensely.

'I want to watch as his *cock* slides into your pussy,' he continued as he spanked her across her behind, her eyes widening as the pleasure and the pain coursed through her body making her moan and open her mouth wide.

'I want to watch as he pounds you hard, and listen as you say his name,' he smacked her again with the flat of his palm and she buried her face in the duvet as she moaned again and wriggled in his grip.

'I want to fuck you, whilst you suck him,' he spanked her harder this time and her head whipped back as she let out a little cry and nodded her head, moaning in agreement.

'I want to hold you close to me and make love to you, as he *fucks* your ass,' he said, smacking her again.

Chapter Two

'Yes,' she said, biting her lip. '*I'd like that.*'

'I want to watch him make you *come*,' he said, moving behind her and undoing his belt.

She heard his trousers drop to the floor beside the bed as he spread her legs, and then she felt her pussy *dripping* in anticipation. 'Fuck me,' she whispered.

'I want to see him fuck you *hard*,' he pushed the head of his cock against her opening and teased her.

'*Please, fuck me,*' she said louder.

And then he pushed forward and slipped inside her.

She felt every beautiful vein and ridge of his cock as her warmth flowered open for him, and somehow it seemed like he was harder and *bigger* than ever before, and after all the build-up, the teasing and the tension of the whole night, she *immediately* began to orgasm, her pussy pulsating and quivering as she shook and writhed on the bed.

Cassian didn't waste any time, thrusting into her again and again, his hand gripping her ass for balance as her pussy pulsed. As her climax gushed through her, she tore at the sheets of the bed and moaned and *moaned* and then she could feel her husband growing inside her as he whispered in her ear. 'And I want to watch as he fills you up like *this*.'

He *roared* aloud as he exploded into her, quicker and harder than he ever had before, pumping rope after rope of love within her lips, shuddering and gasping for breath as the desperation of the moment overcame them both.

'*That's what I want,*' he whispered, leaning over her back, his cock still buried deep inside her, breathing hard as she overflowed. 'That's what I want.'

'I'm going to text them,' said Emilia in a haze of post-orgasmic bliss. 'I'm going to text them *right now.*'

*

CHAPTER THREE

———⋄⋰⋰⋰⋰⋰⋰⋰⋰⋰———

True to her word, Emilia had texted Amy that same night and by the following morning, her new friend had replied, suggesting that they meet up again soon and try a new escape room together that had opened recently in the town centre. The room was one of several in the venue and the one that Amy had suggested was a *horror* one, with a creepy story and a series of clues followed by some role play, but that was all they knew.

Emilia had been reluctant, it wasn't her sort of thing and was rather far outside of her comfort zone, but her excitement about seeing Amy and Mark again had overridden any fear she might have had. Now she and Cassian were in the car, on the way there, and there was very little room for backing out.

'I'm so nervous,' she said as they pulled up into a space two streets away from the venue.

'Don't be, they're another couple, just like us. We're just making new friends.'

Chapter Three

'Yes, but I *like* them,' she said. 'Mark seems really nice, and he's not threatening. He doesn't scare me, and Amy is just stunning, I just want to run my fingers through her hair. I want them to like us, that's why I'm anxious. I want them to like us like I like them, and I'm scared that they won't.'

Cassian took her hand and held it tight. 'Don't walk in there tonight expecting that what we *want* to happen, will happen with *them*, it probably won't. They have no idea what we want, and they probably just want to make friends with us. We should just take it from there and see where it leads.'

'I know,' sighed Emilia, sagging. 'It's just… they're *so* nice.'

Cassian squeezed her hand again and leaned across to kiss her on the cheek. 'Come on, be positive, and enjoy the evening. Maybe Mark will greet us with an armful of pampas grass.'

'*Stop it*,' she said, smiling.

She closed her eyes and opened her door before stepping out into the street. The nighttime air was cold as her husband walked around from the driver's side and took her hand in his, setting off together towards the venue.

She looked up at him, smiling warmly as they walked. 'Shouldn't we say something? Like, drop a hint? Isn't there some sort of code? Like rubbing a knuckle when you shake hands?'

'I'm pretty sure that's the Masons,' he laughed. 'But I'm willing to try.'

'Oh gosh, this is *ridiculous*,' said Emilia, stopping in her tracks and turning back towards the car, head in hands.

'Where are you going?' he called after her.

'I can't do this, it's *too much*.'

'Come on, we're just having a night out with some new friends, take the pressure off.'

She stopped and began to turn around, but as she did so, *Amy* stepped out of the car that was parked right next to her.

'You two okay?' said the enchanting redhead, smiling disarmingly. 'We can rearrange if there's something wrong?'

A moment later Mark stepped out of the driver's side and walked around to the pavement, a concerned look on his face.

Emilia looked at Cassian and smiled, her eyes wild with panic. '*No*, nothing's wrong. Nothing's wrong at all. I just… forgot my purse. It's great to see you both again.'

She stepped forward, took a deep breath, and embraced Amy, kissing her on the cheek and then she did the same again to Mark, who kissed her back before shaking hands with Cassian.

'I've told her she's not allowed to drink this evening, by the way,' laughed Mark, nodding knowingly.

'And I've told *him*, that he's not in charge of what I choose to allow past my *lips*,' pouted Amy as she took Emilia's hand and started walking off up the street. 'I love your shoes,' she said as they stomped away, the two men watching their departure, and sporting wry grins.

The escape room was called *The Doll's House* and on arrival Emilia immediately regretted agreeing to take part. It was situated down a dark alley in the oldest part of the city, which in itself was giving her the creeps.

Upon entering the venue, they were greeted by a theatrical man, dressed up as what appeared to be an old curator or antique shop owner. He approached them rapidly, doddering forward and offering his outstretched and very limp hand, whilst all around them, adorning the walls and shelves, bore down the glass eyes of hundreds and *hundreds* of Porcelain Dolls.

Emilia shivered and gripped Cassian's arm.

'Why hello my dears, and what *beautiful* girls you are, and such handsome gentlemen accompanying you. Why you *must* be Mr and Mrs Black, and Mr and Mrs Hamilton.

Chapter Three

You're so kind to turn up on *time* - I haven't much left you see, so every minute counts. Now, I understand that you're searching for a very *specific* doll for your niece, Mrs Hamilton,' he said to Amy, who blinked. 'I have *just* the one for you, a German Bisque in fact, please follow me, come on through, don't be shy. *You* my boy,' he said to Mark, handing him a box of matches. 'Take these, you may need them if the lanterns blow out. There's a strong wind tonight.'

The couples looked at one another apprehensively. Only Mark seemed unperturbed as he stepped forward, slipping the matches into his pocket and following the curious old man and his fantastical charade further into the darkened shop.

A moment later they stepped through a door into a large candlelit and strangely shaped storeroom. The floor was sloped and the ceiling arched with old beams, and again the eyes of hundreds of dolls stared down at them from every available space, making Emilia shiver.

The man closed the door behind them and there was a small click as it locked. 'Come, *come* we must hurry,' he said ushering them forward into the centre. 'Here she is, here she is,' his enthusiasm difficult to interpret as anything other than genuine. 'Isn't she beautiful? Her name is *Annie*.'

The doll was *grotesque*, half its face was burnt and its clothes were charred and smoke damaged, and as Emilia looked at her she staggered backwards involuntarily, Amy gripping her arm and then holding her hand, momentarily distracting her.

'She has the most unusual story,' the man continued. 'She was sold to me through clearance from the estate of a little girl named Marie, who had been gifted it at a young age by her grandmother. This little girl used to take Annie *everywhere* with her, always talking to her, taking her to bed with her at night, bringing her to the park, sitting her on the swings. To everyone outside the family, Marie was a sweet little girl that seemed to see this wonderful dolly as a little sister. The parents, however, were starting to become worried.'

As the man spoke the lights seemed to flicker, and there came a slow *creak* from upstairs. Amy moved a little closer to Emilia, who gripped hold of her other arm as they embraced.

'Marie would *whisper* to Annie, and Annie would talk back. *Ventriloquism*. At least it seemed that way, the imagination of a child running wild I'm sure, but *Annie* was telling Marie things that she couldn't possibly have known. Family secrets, events that had occurred before she was born, and then Marie began to *do* things, *bad* things. She would tell her parents that Annie had told her to do it. Things like hurting the family dog, setting fire to the rosemary bush out front, putting poison ivy in her father's whisky. Finally, Annie, it seems, told Marie to *throw* herself down the stairs, and the poor little girl broke her leg in the fall.'

Emilia was looking around nervously now, her eyes searching the dolls but not wanting to look too closely as Amy squeezed her hand and whispered, 'It's okay, it's just a story.'

'At this point, the parents decided to rid themselves of the doll, but before they could, Marie started a fire. Sadly, she perished, burnt to death in her own bedroom having never left her bed. And so the parents, childless and heartbroken, sold everything and abandoned the house. I never found out what happened to them, but I was all too happy to buy an immaculate German Bisque. And just look at what *wonderful* condition she's in, like she was born yesterday.'

The old man beamed and held out the burnt, broken doll, the left eye rolling around in its socket and Emilia stepped back, nearly pushing Amy in front of her like a human shield.

Chapter Three

'You're not selling it to me,' laughed Amy, holding Emilia tightly.

Immediately there came a strange noise from above them, a sort of dragging, scraping sound, and the old man looked up quizzically as the two couples followed his gaze, and then there was a sudden gust of wind and the lights went out.

Pitch black.

Mark struck a match and it flared in the darkness and Emilia screamed as all the eyes of the dolls surrounding them reflected the flame and seemed to dance in the shadows, mocking them from the darkness.

And the old man was gone.

But in his place, stood the grotesque doll. It was slowly moving its head to look up at them, and then it pointed and the light of the match flickered out.

Even Mark, the cynic of the group, thought to himself later, that the timing of it all was remarkable.

Both girls *screamed* as Cassian took several steps backwards in fright. Only Mark stayed put, patiently lighting another match from the box.

And the doll was gone.

This time, on the floor in its place, was a handwritten note. Cassian stepped forward, emboldened by Mark's apparent lack of fear, and he coughed before reading it out loud in the light of the flame. 'The collectors time was up and now he's joined Marie. *Annie's coming for you.* You're next. Tick, tock.'

'*Fuck* this,' said Emilia, almost crying as Amy held her shoulders. 'I am *so* scared right now.'

'Why the fuck are we doing this?' said Amy.

'It was your idea,' laughed Cassian.

The candles came back to life as his words echoed, illuminating the room again as Mark looked around. 'Start looking for clues. The note mentioned a clock? Is there a clock amongst the dolls?'

'Are you fucking kidding?' said Emilia. 'Start checking the creepy dolls?'

Cassian laughed. 'This is *awesome*.'

There was another dragging noise from upstairs, and the laughter of a child filtered down from above, then a clock started ticking from somewhere.

'We need to find that clock. Emilia? Do you think you can do that?' said Mark.

'We'll do it together,' said Amy, her breath close and warm.

'It would be faster if we all worked separately?' said mark.

'I am not doing *anything* in here on my own,' snapped Amy.

'Fine,' said Mark before looking over at Cassian. 'Let's see what else we can find.'

The foursome quickly spread out around the room, Amy and Emilia together, holding onto each other as though they were on a life raft, Mark and Cassian searching for anything out of place.

There was a mirror on the far wall and both Amy and Emilia approached it slowly. As they got closer they realised that the ticking sound was coming from *inside*. The mirror had a small lock and some weak looking hinges.

'I think we need to look for a key,' said Amy.

'Any suggestions as to where?' called her husband.

'There's an inscription, in the edge of the frame,' she replied. *'I have no feet to dance, I have no eyes to see, I have no life to live or die but yet I do all three. What am I?'*

Emilia peered up to look, still holding Amy's hand.

'Look for dancing dolls without feet or eyes?' pondered Cassian, shrugging at Mark, but the man was thinking.

'Fire,' he said, as he started to look around, frowning.

'There's another box of matches over here,' said Cassian. 'What's inside?'

Chapter Three

He slid the box open and emptied the contents into his palm. 'A key!'

Emilia's eyes widened and she smiled for the first time as her husband rushed over with it, passing it to her to slide into the lock. She reached up, and clicked it into place, turning it clockwise, but as she did so, the face of *Annie* appeared in the mirror and both girls screamed and fell back.

'Oh fuck, I hate this,' she cried.

Mark stepped forward past the petrified women and opened the cabinet. Inside was a set of rosary beads, but without the traditional cross.

Emilia reached forward. 'Give me those.' She gripped them tightly in her fingers and peered around the room, eyes wide with fear.

Mark looked around the room too, and Cassian followed his gaze.

'I think we have to perform an exorcism to get out?' he said.

'How the hell do you that?' said Amy.

'There must be something we're missing,' said Cass, desperate to contribute, conscious that Mark was doing most of the work and wanting to be more involved.

'We need a Bible, for an exorcism?' he said, not entirely certain, but then the clock stopped and the lights went out once more.

There was that dragging noise again, and Amy screamed, but this time the noise was *closer* - it was *in* the room and the voice of a little girl spoke.

'You can't get rid of me,' she whispered. *'I'm already dead.'*

This time, just *one* of the lights flickered back on, and Amy and Emilia ran to it like moths to a flame, standing wide-eyed and terrified, looking out into the dim darkness, with glass eyes staring back at them from *everywhere*. Even Mark seemed on edge now, and Amy had noticed.

'Why the fuck are we doing this? I don't like it. I don't like it, Mark,' she said, the pair of girls clinging to each other with desperation now.

Cassian came closer and began to look around, and then something caught his eye in the corner of the room. 'Was there a *cot* over there when we came in?'

'Oh fuck *right* off,' said Emilia as she turned to look.

In the corner, where before there had been nothing, there was now an old and rotten rocking cot. It had no mattress or decoration and it was rusted and peeling, and worst of all, it was *moving* as though an unseen hand was gently pushing it.

Inside, very neatly sat on the metal coils of the springs, was a music box, and as they all looked over, it started to play.

'*No, no, no.* I don't like it,' said Amy, shaking her head. 'What do we do?'

Mark didn't move, he seemed to be frozen to the spot, finally past his breaking point. So Cassian walked over to it nervously as Amy and Emilia shuffled forward, peering with morbid curiosity. As he approached, he looked back at Mark, frowning.

'We all have our limits, mate,' he said, staying put.

Cassian nodded and leant over the edge of the cot to pick up the music box. It was still playing but it was winding down slowly. In the bottom was a turn-key to wind it back up, and Cassian realised it was the missing cross for the rosary beads. He pulled at it, and it came out in his hands, the clockwork still whirring and the creepy song still playing.

'Where are those beads?' he called out, and Emilia produced them, still wrapped around her knuckles which were white with fear.

'Amy, can you hook this onto there?'

'Let me see,' she said, and she let go of Emilia's hand.

Then the light went out.

Something brushed past Emilia's leg, and something else

Chapter Three

touched Amy's face and both girls began to scream at once. Then there were voices *everywhere*, as though all the dolls were talking at once.

'*You're worthless,*' they whispered. '*Useless. You can't stop us. Why did you come here? You can't do this. Just give up and die. Die, die, die…*'

The chorus of voices sounded like it was coming from all corners of the room, disorientating them in the darkness.

Mark sparked up another match and Emilia ran over to him like a moth to a flame, closely followed by Amy, both of them holding onto the arms of the now edgy ex-soldier. But Cassian was nowhere to be seen.

'Oh shit, where is he?' said Emilia. 'Where's my husband?'

'I'm *here*,' he said. 'When the voices started, I heard a door open. There's another room back here, but the door closed… and it's now locked.'

Emilia had to admire his bravery. When even Mark was starting to feel unsettled, Cassian had found some reserve of fearlessness, but she found he often did this at home too. If she was upset, he would be calm and rational. If she was sad, he would cheer her up. If she was scared, he would be brave. He was the yin to her yang.

'There's a book on a table, and it's open on a specific page,' he shouted.

'What does it say?' said Mark, approaching the locked door.

'*For it is the power of Christ that compels you, who brought you low by His cross. Tremble before that mighty arm that broke asunder the dark prison walls and led souls forth to light.*'

There was a flash followed by a crash of thunder and a *scream* and then the room plunged into darkness. Mark took a step back and almost stumbled. He had seen Annie, *right* behind Cassian.

The lights didn't come back on.

'Cass, we have to get you out of there, mate,' said Mark.

'The mighty arm that broke asunder the dark prison walls,' he quoted, continuing. 'Can you break down the door?'

'Asunder means to break in two,' said Emilia. 'Does the door fold?'

'It's a barn door,' said Mark, feeling for the latch and releasing it. The bottom section swung open and Cassian crawled through as Mark slammed it shut behind him. 'Did you bring the book?'

'Yep, but how are we gonna read it without light?'

There was another flash of lightning and the girls screamed.

'Give me the fucking rosary beads,' said Amy. '*And* the book. *Who has the cross?*'

Amy was given all the items in quick succession by a myriad of hands in the darkness. Her nerves were tattered, but she was running out of patience. 'Emilia, take the beads,' she fumbled in the darkness for her new friend's hand and squeezed it softly as she handed them to her. 'Hold it out in front of you.'

There was another flash of thunder and she *screamed*. 'She's over there,' she shouted and pointed. '*Annie.*'

They all turned to look and another bright blaze outlined the doll on the floor, standing and staring at them. 'Cass, do you remember what the book said?' she shouted.

'I think so.'

'*Now's* the time.'

'For it is the power of Christ that compels you,' there was a crash of thunder and a scream and then they were surrounded by flames as if the whole room was alight and all the dolls were burning, and in the centre, the burnt figure of Annie - the broken, twisted and demonic doll - was moving slowly toward them.

'For it is the power of Christ that compels you,' Cassian said

Chapter Three

again, and Emilia moved forward with the rosary beads, spurred on by her husband's bravery.

The doll stopped, and there was another piercing *scream* as its mouth opened wide, flames reflected in its eyes.

'For it is the power of Christ that compels you,' said Mark, joining in.

The doll seemed to falter, and then flames began to shoot from *inside* its mouth.

'For it is the power of Christ that *compels you*,' said Amy, holding the book up in front of the doll.

'*For it is the power of Christ that compels you,*' cried Emilia and as soon as she spoke, the flames in the room around them went *out*, leaving the screaming, flaming body of Annie the only source of light - her eyes melting, her mouth falling open, the clothes burning away from her body.

Then, at last, the doll fell onto the floor and the fires went out.

There was a final hiss in the darkness, like gas escaping from a pipe, and then a voice. 'Well done guys, great job.'

Ceiling lights flickered on over their heads and the room was suddenly lit up as bright as day.

'Oh my *fucking* goodness,' said Amy, breathing hard as she stumbled. 'Are you kidding me?'

The door at the far end opened and in walked the old man. 'That was fantastic, well done to you all. If you could follow me out this way, watch your footing? We'll need to start resetting for the next booking soon. If you need to take a minute there's a little room up ahead, and if you want to buy the tape of your adventure it's just twenty pounds per copy.'

Emilia was still shell-shocked and shaking. 'I'm never going to sleep again,' she said before she started laughing somewhat manically. Her giggling caused the others to smile and in turn, they began to laugh too.

After a moment Amy walked over to her and hugged her

tight, and Emilia hugged her back, squeezing her hard as though she might run away. They both felt like they had been through some sort of battle and come out the other side, stronger for it.

'Good work, mate,' said Mark to Cassian, slapping him on the shoulder. 'You'd have made a cracking soldier.'

Slowly, they started to make their way towards the door, Amy holding Emilia's hand, swinging it back and forth in triumph.

In the next room were four cups of herbal tea, freshly made and steaming, and as they crossed the threshold, a young lady appeared behind them and invited them to settle themselves down and take a moment to breathe and relax and enjoy the brew. 'It's all part of the experience,' she said as she left them alone.

'That was *too* scary,' said Emilia after a sip of the tea.

'I have never been so scared in all my life,' said Amy.

'I've had worse moments,' said Mark. 'But not many.'

'Shit, I think I understand what you used to talk about now,' said Amy, sipping gently. 'About going through a firefight with someone, how you bond with them. I feel like we all just went through an intense shared experience and we're now *bonded* for life.'

She laughed, but there was a part of her that meant it. Everything had seemed much too real, right up until the moment the lights went on.

'Thank you,' said Emilia, reaching out her hand for Amy's again. 'You looked after me in there.'

'I wasn't looking after you, I was petrified and you were my *crutch*,' she laughed. 'I would have sacrificed you without a second thought if that fucking doll got any closer.'

Emilia feigned shock and laughed.

'Fine, I would've missed you *terribly*,' said Amy winking.

'Cass was a *badass*,' said Mark, his new friend visibly

Chapter Three

humbled by this suggestion.

'Thanks, mate. It was fun.'

'Fun? *Fun?*' said Emilia. 'I don't even know you right now. *Who are you?*'

'Shall we get going? I'm hungry,' said Amy, standing up. 'Table's booked for eight so we should start walking.'

'I'm not sure I can eat food after that,' said Emilia. 'But let's give it a shot.'

*

The restaurant was a fifteen-minute walk from the escape room, but it felt like further after what they had all been through. Emilia was edgier than usual and was clinging to Cassian's arm as they walked up to the entrance of Picollito's, the small Italian pizzeria that Mark had chosen and booked for them. A pretty young waitress greeted them at the door and led them to a circular table overlooking the plaza outside, and as they all drew near, Cassian pulled out two chairs for the two girls before he and Mark settled down next to them.

'Mark, I have *no idea* how you managed to not drop-kick that little-shit puppet, Annie out of the fucking room? I mean what kind of bodyguard *are you* if you can't keep me safe from a possessed porcelain doll?'

The waitress raised her eyebrows in confusion and left the table swiftly, abandoning them with one less menu than intended, resulting in Amy and Emilia having to share.

'So where do you guys live?' said Amy as she perused the menu.

'South of the city, on the new estate.'

'The one near the motorway?'

'That's the one,' said Emilia, smiling.

'You're a physiotherapist and he's in marketing? You guys must be raking it in.'

'We're saving,' said Cassian.

'For kids?'

Emilia nodded. 'So how did you get started making *shit art?*'

Amy laughed hard, throwing her head back, and Emilia watched, rapt, as her long red hair fell gracefully around her neck.

'You're such a *bitch*,' she grinned. 'Honestly? It was an accident. I was working at a gallery in Switzerland, eight years ago. There was an exhibition about mundanity, all that rubbish about focusing on the boring objects that surround us and elevating them to be observed thereby creating some sort of bullshit paradox. Well, I was told to go mop the gallery floor one night by our manager. As they were closing up, one of the last tourists had *literally* shit their pants. I don't know the full story, but the next thing I knew, I was given a mop and bucket and told to go clean up. As I was walking through this gallery of *shit* art, I decided right then and there, that I was done. I kicked the bucket of water onto the poo, threw the mop on top, went and found a marker pen and wrote *The Life of Amy Hamilton* on the floor and threw the pen aside. The next day it was in the newspaper. One of the local press critics had a late-night viewing and the curator just assumed I'd cleaned up the turd, but the critic loved it. So to answer your question, I got started making shit art, by making *shit art*.'

'That is amazing,' said Emilia. 'If you ever write a biography, that should be your opening paragraph.'

Amy raised her middle finger at Emilia as they laughed. 'So now you know my dark past, and that I'm literally *full of poop*,' said Amy. 'Tell me about *you guys*. Every time I've asked anything approaching a personal question, you've managed to dodge, I'm starting to wonder if you're fugitives, or spies, or in witness protection or something.'

Chapter Three

'You're right, we should tell them the truth, Em,' said Cassian, feigning suspicion and looking around nervously.

'*No, you promised me you wouldn't,*' she laughed, pretending to admonish him as she played along. 'We *can't* tell them, their lives would be in danger.'

'Not with me around,' said Mark, calmly.

Cassian had noticed that their new friend had positioned himself facing the door and his chair was angled slightly toward the fire exit. He had also shifted the table a few inches when they'd sat down. He had wondered if this was conscious or just such an ingrained part of Mark's life that he did it everywhere he went.

'You have no excuse now,' said Amy, drumming the table with her fingers. '*Spill.* What's the dark secret?'

Emilia glanced over at Cassian who nodded.

'It's nothing exciting I'm afraid, we just met at school.'

'How old are you guys?' frowned Amy.

Mark coughed politely. 'As I'm sure you're aware by now, Amy doesn't know how to ask polite questions.'

'You've been together since you were *teenagers?*' said Amy.

Emilia nodded, a little nervously. She hadn't really wanted this to come up.

'That's so *lovely,*' said her friend.

Cassian squeezed Emilia's hand across the table. 'Thank you.'

'So have you ever been with anyone *else?*'

Mark looked over at his wife disapprovingly as Emilia glanced toward Cassian, feeling a little uncomfortable. This question had come up a few times in their lives, and it was impossible to answer satisfactorily.

'No,' said Cassian. 'Just each other.'

There was a brief silence around the table, which Amy broke. 'That's so romantic.'

Emilia relaxed a little.

'I can't imagine that,' she continued and was about to say something else, but the waitress interrupted them to ask for their order and Amy forgot for the time being what she was going to say, and by the time they had finished their main course, there had been so many other conversations, that Emilia felt they were reasonably safe from the usual probing and personal comments.

'We need to have pudding,' said Amy, a little tipsy after her third glass of wine. 'You have to try the lemon sorbet, it's literally the *best* I've ever had.'

'Lemon sorbet?' said Emilia.

'*I know*, but honestly, they must have some secret ingredient here that elevates it to a different level.'

'Okay,' said Emilia, smiling wide. 'I trust you.'

A short while later, the waitress brought over a large bowl of sorbet, topped with ice cream, coated with whipped cream, and sprinkled with chocolate and then laid out four spoons.

'Hang on, wait,' said Amy to Emilia, grabbing one of the spoons. 'Try the sorbet first.'

She leaned forward and dug into the depths of the bowl and came back with a small spoon of glistening yellow ice and then she brought it up to Emilia's lips with reverence. 'Go on, try it.'

She opened her mouth and Amy slipped the spoon inside, the sorbet melting onto her tastebuds, and then she wiped the corner of Emilia's mouth with her thumb, making her tingle and taking her breath away.

Amy was right, the sorbet was amazing, but the delivery was *heaven*.

*

Half an hour later the two girls stumbled out of the restaurant, holding hands and laughing and almost falling

Chapter Three

into the street.

'Careful love,' said a passing man as Amy nearly knocked him over.

'*Sorry*,' she called after him as he walked on past, then she burst into laughter again. It had started to rain since finishing their meal, and the street was slick with water, the multi-coloured reflections of the neon signs and headlights that surrounded them mixing like an oil painting in the puddles. 'Oh my goodness, I have had the *best* night, Em. Can I call you, Em? Oh, you're like that miserable woman in those spy films. Em. Em.'

Emilia laughed and held her friend upright, putting one arm around her waist and the other on her shoulder.

'You are so fucking beautiful, Emily,' continued Amy. 'Emilia. Gosh, I could just *kiss you*.'

'*Go on then*,' she said, daring her. The men came out behind them a moment later, closing the big glass door and joining their wives in the street as they all started to walk and stumble in the direction of their cars.

'I have had *such* an amazing night with you guys,' said Amy, now walking hand in hand with Emilia again. 'It was the most *terrifying* night of my life, and I'm going to have to sleep with the light on for the next six *months* and burn *all* of my dolls, but it was *amazing*.'

'You have dolls?' said Emilia.

'Don't ask,' said Amy. 'I won't after tonight in any case,' then she slipped her hand up Emilia's arm and hooked it over her elbow. 'We must do this again soon,' she continued. 'Not the Doll's House, I'm never setting foot in there again. But going out together, and not in a *We must do this again soon, but not really* way, but actually, very soon, we should go out again together and have some more fun. Maybe bowling or wine tasting. You know, something that doesn't involve being scarred for life.'

'We should, it's been really nice,' said Emilia, smiling at their new friends as her heart thumped in her chest.

'There's one question I still have about you and Cass, though,' said Amy, and Emilia cringed waiting to hear it, knowing what was coming. 'Haven't you *ever* wanted to sleep with anyone else?'

'That's enough,' said Mark.

'No I'm just curious,' she said. 'I'm not being mean. I just, like, how do you know it's *good?* You know, *fucking?* If you haven't shagged anyone else but each other?'

'Come back to ours then,' said Emilia, suddenly and seriously.

Amy stopped walking.

Mark and Cassian walked past and then stopped a few paces further on.

For a moment, Amy laughed, and then her expression changed. She looked at Emilia and frowned. 'You're serious aren't you?'

Emilia didn't respond. Mark looked over at Cassian and back towards the girls but said nothing.

'No, of course, I'm not serious,' said Emilia, feigning laughter. She looked nervously at Cassian, begging him to back her up.

'You are serious, and you're a *shit* liar. Is this what tonight was about for you guys? Make friends and then try and see if you can get us into bed?'

Emilia looked petrified under Amy's ire.

Cassian walked up behind his wife and put an arm on her back gently.

'No, I just-' said Emilia, deflated and confused.

'Mark, I think we need to go now,' said Amy and she turned to cross the street. A car honked its horn and swerved around her as it drove by, a fine mist of water spraying up from its tyres.

Chapter Three

Emilia looked on as the rain came down, watching as Amy's heels clicked away across the road.

Mark stood awkwardly and then turned to Cassian. 'It was great to see you guys again, sorry,' he said, setting off after his wife and turning back briefly. 'Thanks.'

He continued after her at a slow jog, his feet splashing in the surface water as he went. Emilia watched as they got into their car, pulled out and drove off down the street. Amy turned her face away as they slew past.

Gently, Cassian put his arm around his wife and held her kindly as she stood still, her eyes wide and hurt, as Mark and Amy's car drove around the corner and disappeared from sight.

'Come on Em, you're getting soaked. Let's go home.'

*

'Cass I'm so sorry,' said Emilia. 'I fucked up.'

'Yes you did,' he said, putting the car into first gear and pulling away from the curb.

'Should I text her?'

'No, definitely not.'

'Oh gosh, I feel sick.'

'Don't be sick in the car,' he snapped somewhat unsympathetically before slowing down.

Emilia leaned forward, her head in her hands as she started to cry. 'I'm sorry,' she said. 'I shouldn't have said that. I should've just listened to you.'

Cassian closed his eyes and breathed. 'It's fine Em, you said something silly in the heat of the moment, after a few too many drinks. You didn't mean it. We can square this away. It's fine.'

'It's not fine though, I like her and I like him. It's like I'm *fourteen* again. I've got butterflies in my tummy and I feel like

I just asked you out all over again but you said *no*. I *really* like her. I'm going to text them.'

'Don't, not yet.'

'Why not?'

'Just leave it for now. Leave them alone,' he said, more forcefully than intended. 'Planned or not, you've put the idea out there now. If the shoe was on the other foot, then we might be upset at first, but then we might talk about it.'

Emilia blinked and looked up, hopeful. 'Do you think?'

'I don't know.'

'Are you just saying this to cheer me up?'

'Yes and no. Just leave them to think about it. Mark approached me in the toilets of the mansion and started up a conversation because he'd caught me checking out his *wife*.'

'You didn't tell me that before,' said Emilia, wiping tears from her eyes.

'The point is, they might walk away and think about it and wonder if we were serious,' he said, turning onto the motorway, the dull yellow lights fading in and out across the dashboard as they passed under the tall lamps. 'And if you text them now and apologise and say you were joking or whatever, then it shuts it down for good. Just leave them alone.'

'I'm so sorry,' she said again.

'It's fine, *we're* fine. I love you.'

'I love you too,' she leaned across and placed her hand on top of his. 'I had a nice time tonight.'

Cass took another deep breath and then half-smiled. 'I did too.'

By the time they got home, Emilia had fallen asleep, so Cassian picked her up and carried her inside the house and up the stairs to bed.

He took off her shoes and caressed her feet, squeezing them warmly, and then he unzipped her dress and slipped it off from around her shoulders. Then, with a careful reverence, he lifted her up and helped her underneath the covers, kissing her on the forehead and tucking her in.

Finally, with a deep and satisfied sigh, he undressed and gradually shut down the house, hanging up his wife's dress, turning out the lights - with a slight shiver of irrational doll induced fear - cleaning his teeth and straightening out his jacket.

By the time he got into bed, Emilia was awake again, her cheeks wet with tears. 'Will you make love to me?' she said, softly.

'Of course,' he said and he leaned in, and kissed her full on the lips.

*

CHAPTER FOUR

Emilia spent the following day trying to keep herself busy, although she could barely concentrate. She kept replaying the conversation over and over again in her head, exploring different ways it might have gone - picturing scenarios where Amy kissed her in the rain like a scene from a movie, and others where they argued and never spoke again.

She spent time thinking about what she would say if they were to see each other, and how that might play out, with her persuading Amy and Mark to just give it a try, with no pressure. She was so inside her own head it had taken her a few minutes to realise that she had gone into the kitchen three times to pour herself a glass of water and had forgotten to do so on each attempt.

Cassian had gone into work that morning and Emilia had envied him, he was better at dealing with anxiety and he was *out*, doing his job, distracted and focused. She'd thought for some time if she should do the same, maybe by swapping

Chapter Four

shifts with someone, but then she ran the risk of bursting into tears during an appointment or in the break room, and she quickly changed her mind.

Every now and again she felt her heart ache inside her chest, as though it was heavy with sadness or loss. At other times she felt overcome with a heightened sense of awareness and nervousness and would frequently check her phone. She even began to hear phantom text message noises, she was so desperate to hear *something* from them.

Having cleaned the house, vacuumed, mopped, wiped the mirrors and scrubbed all the bathrooms - in case they came round - she decided she should sit down and read, to try and take her mind away to another place. But after six or seven failed attempts to even finish a single page, she sat and cried.

She had become too excited, too quickly. Why had she even thought this would work out? The first couple they'd met? *Really?* She still wasn't really sure if this was what Cassian wanted either. Had she honestly thought that meeting another couple with the same mindset as them would be so simple?

Yes. *She had.*

And not only had she thought that, but she had fallen for Amy *hard*, just like Alice had said she would. She'd had crushes before, once in college and a couple of times at work - both of which she'd told Cassian about - but *never* like this. She *yearned* for Amy - they had a connection, and it was more than just friendship, there was chemistry there. It all hinged on whether she felt the same. And it was becoming swiftly apparent, that she didn't.

After a while her sobs began to subside and her tears began to dry. She wanted to text or call her so much it hurt. She wanted to hear her voice and see her face, but she knew it was crazy, and that she would come across as some sort of stalker.

She remembered reading once that you should never text or call someone you like whilst horny. The article was meant for men, but the recommendation was to masturbate before calling someone for a shag, and if you still wanted to afterwards, then it was probably a good idea. It was a bit like not going shopping when you were hungry. So she gathered herself together, went upstairs to the bedroom and lay down on her bed. Then she rested her cheek on her pillow and slipped her hand inside her knickers.

She couldn't help it. *Immediately* she started picturing herself and Cassian, and Mark and Amy, together in their bedroom.

She saw herself kissing Amy, taking off her dress, caressing her breast, hand against her crotch, feeling Mark behind her, feeling Cassian's hand on her stomach, her arms, her ass, all of them warm and soft, skin against skin. Mark fucking her, Cassian fucking Amy.

It was like her own personal version of her naughty book. Except the Duke was Mark, and Amy was Elizabeth.

She felt herself climax quickly. It wasn't a great orgasm, it was dirty and rushed, but it felt different to usual... more taboo, more forbidden, more *intense* somehow. She needed this, more than she had realised.

As her senses returned, she checked her phone again.

No new messages.

But at least now she knew.

She *liked* them. *Both* of them. Mostly Amy, but she knew she could easily grow to like Mark more and more. He was a real gentleman like Cassian, and a real man too.

She'd *come*, and she still wanted to text.

She opened up her messaging app and began to write.

Hi Amy, I'm sorry about how the other night ended. It was just a joke, I hope you didn't take it serio-

Chapter Four

* * *

She deleted what she'd written, tapping the backspace over and over and trying not to accidentally press send. There was no point in lying. That wasn't going to get her anywhere.

Hi Amy, I'm sorry. I like you, and Mark. We like you. Even if you don't like us back, I still want to be your friend x

She read it back to herself. It still wasn't completely honest, but it was better. She didn't want to be *just friends* with Amy, but she would settle for that if she had to, and keep looking for someone else, and hope that over time her feelings would subside.

She hovered over the send button, but couldn't bring herself to press it.

Instead, she tapped on the back button, opened her contacts and called Alice.

*

'So let me get this straight,' said Alice. 'You went to the ball, you fell in love with the Prince and the Princess, you invited them out on a *date* - which they didn't know about - and then you asked them to come back to your place for a four-way?'

Emilia nodded, chewing her lip.

'*Nice*,' said Alice raising her brow. 'But it didn't go to plan?'

Emilia shook her head.

'And now you're blubbing like a teenage girl at a boy band concert.'

'And my vagina is just as hysterical,' said Emilia.

Alice laughed. 'At least you haven't lost your humour… Now, I don't mean to state the obvious, but did you subtly establish if they were into partner swapping first? You know, *before* you blurted it out?'

'They were at the Masquerade.'

'Did they go to the *fucking other people* part? This is important.'

Emilia shook her head.

'The fact that they *didn't* should have been a clue,' said her sister as she sat back.

'So what do I do?' said Emilia.

'What *can* you do? You can't *make* someone like you. The same goes for normal relationships.'

'But I like them.'

'You're going to have to unlike them. There's a saying some pretentious asshole once told me; you can make swingers into friends, but you can't make friends into swingers. Now *I'm* the pretentious asshole. It's like a gift that keeps on giving. You made the mistake of making friends first.'

Emilia nodded as Alice continued.

'It's like dating. You don't go up to someone and say, *Hey, can I be your friend? Maybe later I'll want to fuck you, and by then it might be confusing and inappropriate, but let's start off by just being supportive of one another in a platonic way,'* she said, grinning.

Emilia laughed now, wiping her wet cheek with the back of one hand. 'But I've never dated anyone except Cass,' she said.

'Oh *shit*, this is *my* fault,' said Alice. 'I didn't even *think* about the fact that you don't have the first fucking clue about dating.'

Emilia smiled and looked down into her lap. Instead of ruminating over texting Amy, she had texted her sister and asked her to come round as soon as she could, and within seconds Alice had responded by writing *Why? Is The Greek finally up for some ass? Xx*

Chapter Four

An hour later she had pulled into the driveway with a bottle of milk, some of Emilia's favourite chocolates and a loving hug. Now they were sat together in the conservatory - which Alice had once described as *fucking pointless, it's either too hot in the summer or too cold in the winter, and full of fucking spiders the rest of the time* - next to each other, on a couple of rattan chairs that Emilia had arranged around a glass table, the doors open to the outside, with a pleasant breeze and a spot of sunshine, and even Alice couldn't deny that it was rather nice. 'It's just common sense, sweetie,' she continued.

'I know,' said Emilia, huffing and rubbing her temple. 'Would you like another cup of tea?'

'There's not much tea can't fix, so yes,' said Alice, holding out her cup.

Emilia went through to the kitchen and shuffled around before calling through the hatch. 'Did you go to the ball? I didn't see you there.'

'That's the idea.'

'I know but I thought I would've noticed you, or heard you.'

'I kept my distance, well, from you at least. Cass has a *seriously* tight ass though.'

Emilia dropped the spoon she was using to stir the tea. 'That was you?'

'He mentioned me did he?' said Alice, laughing.

Emilia brought the tea through. 'It came up, *yes*,' Emilia said, smiling for the first time since she'd arrived. 'Thank you. I'm sorry I've brought you into my mess. I don't know what I'm doing,' she sat down again. 'I'm so confused and it feels really weird talking to you about this, but I really like them.'

'Does Cass feel the same way?'

'I think so, but he's better at emotions than me. He can handle this, he's rational and calm and he doesn't get overwhelmed or anxious.'

She closed her eyes and breathed deeply.

Alice leaned forward and took her sister's hand, squeezing it. 'Hey, it's gonna be okay.'

'I just feel sad.'

'It's normal. You're experiencing all the shitty, depressing emotions that everybody else around you went through when they were between thirteen and twenty-three. Except you're experiencing them ten years too late. You never got a handle on rejection. This is the first time someone you fancied said *no*.'

Emilia nodded. 'There was Peter in year five,' she smiled through a glaze of tears.

'That doesn't count,' said Alice. 'Peter thought you were going to give him *kissing disease* if he said yes. The point is, this is *new* to you. It's going to take a little time to get over and you need to give yourself that time. *Heal*, then make sure your relationship is okay, and then start again if that's what you want.'

'You're so good at this,' said Emilia.

Alice shrugged. 'Mum always told us to play the field. I just listened.'

'She said the field, not the football team.'

'Bitch,' she grinned.

'So what should I do now?'

'Leave it. Cassian is right. If there's something there, then they will text you back. If not, they will earmark you as the swinging weirdos and give you a wide berth at every function you both attend from now on.'

Emilia nodded and drank some more of her tea.

'Listen, I know I'm always running off, but I really do have to dash,' said Alice. 'I've got to finish a client's annual report and I'm probably going to have to pull an all-nighter to do it, so I want to get started if that's okay?'

Chapter Four

'Of course,' said Emilia, standing up, after a brief but awkward moment where she tried not to burst into tears again, she walked her sister to the front door and they hugged farewell.

'Don't text her,' said Alice. 'Promise?'

Emilia sneered and laughed guardedly. 'I'll try.'

'Or do, because you're an adult and you can do what you like,' she said, as she walked away towards her car.

Emilia stood in the doorway watching as her sister pulled out of the driveway and waved as she dipped down onto the main road. Then she turned around, closed the door and headed back to the kitchen, picking up her phone.

Quickly, she sat back down in the conservatory and tapped on Amy's name.

Hi Amy, can we meet? I really want to talk to you x

Honest and to the point, she thought to herself.

She pressed send and put the phone down on the glass coffee table, then she closed her eyes and slowly exhaled.

She'd done it. Now all she had to do was wa-

Brrrrr.

The little table vibrated so loudly she thought the glass might break.

Panic rose in her chest. Was it Amy, already? If so, it probably wasn't good. Something heartbreaking like *Lose my number*. Or perhaps it was Alice or Cass? Just a coincidental text to say *Thanks* or *On my way home x*.

She stared at her phone for a long time, paralysed, too scared to look, but eventually, she rationalised and settled herself down, reached forward for it, and read Amy's name, and the short message below.

Hinksey Park? 3 pm? X

* * *
*

Emilia had thrown on the best outfit she could find at short notice and bundled her hair up into a messy ponytail as her heart had tried its best to escape her chest. Hinksey Park was six stops away on the number thirty-five and by running she'd managed to make it just in time for the next departure. Now she was sat down near the front, phone in hand and half an hour to spare before Amy would be there.

She decided that the first thing she would do would be to make a custom text message alert for her new friend. Every time her phone buzzed, she would become instantly anxious, wondering if it was her. This way, she would know straight away and could take things a little more easily throughout the day. She selected one called *Bird Song* and put away her phone, then she looked out of the window as they passed over the railway bridge on Old Abingdon Road, watching as a train shot by beneath her.

What were they doing? What were they going to talk about? Was Amy going to tell her to leave them alone? To lose her number and stop contacting her?

She wasn't sure if she could take that. It wasn't likely though, was it? She'd invited her to meet, it would be pretty brutal to crush her face to face. Not impossible though.

Fifteen agonising minutes later the bus began to slow down and Emilia stood up and pressed the stop button, holding on tight as it came to a sharp halt next to a small shelter. She looked around nervously, suddenly afraid that Amy might be on the same bus, or just about to walk past outside. She needed a bit more time to prepare before she saw her again, she wasn't quite ready yet.

'You getting off, love?' said the driver.

'Oh, sorry,' she said. She made her way forward quickly,

feeling the stares of some of the other passengers, and then she stepped down onto the curb and hopped away before turning to say thank you, but the driver was already pulling away.

The entrance to the park was a short walk from the stop, and she set off in the right direction, head down and deep in thought, her mind preoccupied with thoughts about what Amy might say; about the other night; about what might happen in the future; about how her new friend was never going to want to see her again. She was mortified and terrified, but most of all she felt sad, and before she realised it, she was part of the way along the path that led around the lake.

There was a little bench up ahead that looked out over the water and sitting on it was a red-haired girl. From this distance, she wasn't sure if it was her but as she got closer, the girl turned her head and smiled and Emilia could see now that it was Amy and her heart started to flutter. She stood up as she drew near.

'Hi,' she said, chewing her lip and tilting her head.

'Hi,' said Emilia.

Then they both started to speak at once, a jumbled combination of *how are you*'s and *I'm fine's*. Amy looked down at the floor, embarrassed but smiling.

'Do you want to take a walk?' she said, before nodding toward the path to her left.

'I'd like that,' said Emilia.

For a few minutes, they walked in silence, not really looking at each other, just glancing around at the sights and sounds of the park, and yet despite everything, it felt *comfortable* and Emilia found herself wishing they could hold hands.

A young mum and dad were playing with their little girl off to the side and their pink ball rolled past Emilia's feet, heading toward the lake. She scooped it up in her hands quickly and then rolled it back gently toward the little girl who smiled brightly.

'That was nice of you,' said Amy, smiling. 'You'll be a good mum, one day.'

Emilia smiled at her briefly and then looked away across the lake at the ducks. 'I'm sorry,' she said.

'There's nothing to be sorry about,' said Amy. 'I've just never had a girl tell me she likes me before.'

'I've never *liked* a girl before,' said Emilia.

Amy smiled. 'I like you,' she said with a pained smile. 'But I don't know if I like you like *that*.'

Emilia's heart thudded as Amy's words washed over her and for a fearful second, she thought she might burst into tears. Instead, she took a long staccato breath and after a moment they started walking again, not saying anything. She had known what Amy was going to say, from the moment she'd received her text message, but it still hurt to hear it.

As they walked, she felt like a small crack had formed in her heart. She wasn't heartbroken, she still loved Cassian and he still loved her, but the part of her heart that had grown for Amy and Mark, was now damaged and it was going to take some time to heal.

Amy stopped by the bridge that ran between the two small lakes, and rested her elbows on the railing, looking out over the water.

'Isn't it beautiful here?' she said. Emilia followed her gaze and then looked back at Amy, her red hair drifting gently in the breeze as she continued. 'Mark proposed here, right over there,' she said, pointing to the spot.

'I want you,' Emilia said suddenly. 'And Mark. We both do.'

'You can't just say that,' said Amy. 'It's not fair.'

'Why not?'

Chapter Four

'It's not *right* either.'

'Then why did you agree to meet me?'

Amy hesitated. 'I don't know,' she looked down at the water running below them and then back up at Emilia. 'I'm confused,' she said, at last.

Emilia said nothing, waiting for her friend to talk.

'I'm confused because everything was- *is*, normal. Mark and I love each other, we have a life together, we're talking about kids, saving money, selling our cars, remortgaging, buying a new washing machine. All that normal, boring, *life* stuff, and then we met you guys and you just threw a spanner in it all.'

'Why does that have to be a bad thing?'

'It doesn't,' said Amy. 'But it's *different*. I don't know, I don't know how to explain it.'

She turned to keep walking and Emilia followed, moving up beside her. 'I mean let's just say we all fucked. Then what? You want more than that, don't you?'

'Maybe,' said Emilia, her heart now racing.

'I don't know if I can give you that, or if *we* can give you that, and that's too much *pressure*. What next? Move in together? Start a family? We *can't* do that. It won't work.'

'I don't know,' said Emilia, tears starting to form in her eyes, the crack in her heart felt like it was growing now and she bit her lip as more tears began to flow.

Amy turned around, facing her. They had stopped beneath a willow tree on a bend, and Emilia could hear the birds singing in the branches above as the sunlight dappled through the leaves and danced on the wooded path they stood upon.

It was beautiful.

For a long moment they both looked at each other, their eyes glistening with emotion, and then Amy took Emilia's hand, and leaned in, and *kissed* her.

It started soft, just a peck, and then the palm of her hand was on her cheek, her thumb brushing her ear, and then they were kissing each other deeply and urgently as Emilia's mind went into a haze, as though everything had turned down in volume and become numb.

Oh gosh. Yes.

She put her hand up into Amy's hair and run her fingers through it, her skin tingling with desire, her heart healing in seconds and growing, but as soon as she did, her new friend pulled *away*, and before she could process what was happening, she was walking off, *fast*.

Emilia went to follow, still dizzy from their kiss, but Amy just kept going, almost *running* back up the path.

She called out to her. 'Amy?'

'I'm sorry,' she said, and then she was gone around the corner.

Emilia stood under the tree and touched her lips, still able to feel the warmth of Amy's kiss upon them.

Then the tears really started to flow, as her heart broke in two.

*

When Cassian arrived home, Emilia was making dinner for both of them. There were pots and pans all over the kitchen surfaces, and whilst she had done her best to make a full home-cooked meal, she wasn't the most organised cook. At the best of times she was scatty and forgetful and getting timings right was always a challenge for her, and today was far worse than usual, but Cassian loved her all the more for trying. He wrapped his arms tightly around her waist and kissed her on the cheek, coming away with what looked and *felt* like raw egg on his lips. He laughed and wiped it aside and then squeezed her again.

Chapter Four

'Don't be mad,' she said, turning around and putting her arms around his neck.

'Why? What have you done?'

She looked up into his eyes nervously and he frowned back.

'What is it?' he said.

'I might have messaged Amy,' she said.

Cassian's expression froze. 'And?'

'We met up.'

His eyes widened. 'What happened?'

'We… talked,' she looked down at his chest. 'And… we *kissed*.'

'*Oh*,' he said, still holding her.

'Are you angry?'

'No, not at all. What's wrong though? You look upset.'

'She left after we kissed. She was… confused,' said Emilia. 'And she said that this isn't what she wants.'

'Oh, I'm sorry Em,' he hugged her tightly and felt her shake as she started to cry into his chest. 'Maybe it just wasn't meant to be.'

He stroked her hair as she nodded. 'I'm sorry,' she said. 'It's like Alice said, I fall quickly, just look at you and me.'

She sniffed as she continued. 'I fell for you when I was fourteen. What the hell does a fourteen-year-old know? It's not like I made the wrong decision, I was just lucky it was you.'

Cassian shrugged as she went on. 'I just, I wanted this to happen, and I didn't think it would, and then it looked like it might and I fell for her. I didn't think I would fall, not that quickly. But I fucking *did*. And I think she likes me, and us, too, because she kissed me. But she doesn't know what she wants.'

She stopped, trying to calm herself, breathing in and out. '*Fuck*, this is hard,' she said at last. 'I didn't think it was going to be this hard.'

'I know.'

A sudden smell of burning started to make her nose twitch and she looked around, confused. 'Oh shit, *dinner*.'

She rushed over to the oven and opened the door to a billow of black smoke and a very chargrilled pasta bake. In despair, she sat down on the floor with a bump and leaned back against the cupboard door, putting her head in her hands and sobbing. 'I'm sorry, I'm sorry, I'm *so sorry*,' she repeated.

'Hey, *hey*,' said Cassian. 'It's fine, we can fix this.'

'Fix what? The dinner or me?'

'Both,' he said, his voice turning stern. 'Come on, up. Stand up.'

He took hold of her hands and pulled her upright, then turned off the oven. Then he grabbed the mitts, slipped them on and plucked the burning pasta bake out of the oven, taking it out into the garden to cool down.

When he came back in, Emilia was upright but leaning against the counter again, her eyes closed.

'Come with me,' he said. Taking her arm, he guided her through to the lounge, scooping up their tablet computer on the way. 'I'll order takeout.'

He sat her down on the couch, then plonked down beside her and opened the little device, browsing to the website of a nearby curry restaurant that offered delivery and racked up their usual order. Then he pulled her in closer to him and lay her head down on his chest and cuddled her, closing his own eyes as she quietly wept.

Twenty minutes later the doorbell rang, startling her awake as Cassian stood up to answer, retrieving their food from the front door and heading into the kitchen to plate it all up.

'Are we doing the right thing?' she said, standing in the

Chapter Four

doorway and rubbing her eyes.

'I don't know,' he said as he stopped tipping curry from the takeout pot onto the plate for a moment and leaned back.

'I feel like all this has just created upset and sadness and disappointment, and it's my fault,' said Emilia.

He ran his hands under the tap and dried them and then approached his wife, arms outstretched to hold her. 'It's okay, we'll get through this. It was our first try, we can learn from this and move on.'

'That's just it though, maybe the lesson is that we *shouldn't* do this. Everyone else does fine as a couple, and I *am* happy with you. I was happy before this. I love you. I'm sorry.'

'I love you too,' he said.

For a little while, they held each other in the kitchen, embracing and squeezing each other, until Cassian pulled back and spoke. 'I'm guided by you. If you want to keep trying then we will, if you want to stop, we stop, if you want to pause and think, we pause and think, but right now our curry is getting cold, so let's eat.'

Emilia smiled, took a long deep breath, and said. 'Thank you.'

But she couldn't stop thinking about that kiss.

*

Fifteen minutes later, they were scraping their plates and watching evening television, sitting side by side. Emilia was cross-legged, her plate on her knees with half of her attention on the show they were watching and the other half still processing and replaying her kiss with Amy.

Cassian was yawning and leaning back on the couch and his wife was chomping on her last piece of poppadom when her phone buzzed and a second later, the sound of bird song drifted softly through the room.

She froze like a deer in the headlights, her mouth slowly falling open as her heart raced.

Cassian looked over at her, then at the phone and frowned. 'What's wrong?' he said.

She was rooted to the couch, too nervous to get up and read the message. It could *only* have been from Amy, she had set that message tone herself.

She bit her lip and stood unsteadily, a nauseating feeling of trepidation growing in the pit of her stomach, making her feel sick as she moved. She walked over to the phone as her husband watched, and picked it up, the message obscured until she pressed her finger against the reader, then she took a deep breath and tapped.

Hi, it's Amy. I'm sorry I took off earlier. I was just a bit overwhelmed. We had such a great time with you, both of you. I really like you. So does Mark. Can we see you both again? Spa day? The Aurora? Saturday morning? No pressure XxxX

Emilia smiled and breathed in so much and so deeply that Cassian thought she might pass out. Then she laughed and wiped a small tear away from her eye.

'What is it?' he said. 'What does it say?'

'See for yourself,' she said, passing him the phone.

He read it, then read it again and half-frowned, half-smiled. 'So…'

She reached in to take her phone back. 'What do you think it means?'

'I don't know,' he said. 'I'm not sure I want to speculate.'

'But she says *I really like you*, not *let's just be friends* - surely that means something?'

'I think she's being careful?' he said, after some consideration.

Chapter Four

'And she says *both of you*, and *so does Mark*,' Emilia's excitement was palpable now as she began to pace and spin.

'Don't overreact,' he said. 'They might have just decided we're worth being friends with anyway. Which is really nice, but that's not what you want.'

'But you didn't hear what she was *saying* earlier, and look at the sign-off,' she said, pointing to the message again. 'Four kisses? Two big, two small? Come on, that's intentional, that's like a hidden message or something. You don't *accidentally* type that.'

'Or her hand slipped? Or she hasn't put that much thought into it?' said Cassian, trying to temper his increasingly hyped up and overexcited wife. 'We don't know for sure. Can we even make this weekend?'

'Whatever is in the calendar is *cancelled*,' she said, still fretting. 'What do you even *wear* to a spa? Shit, what do I text back? Oh fuck *I have to text her back*. I am *so shit* at dating.'

She laughed again, but it was happy excitable laughter.

'Don't text back straight away,' he said raising his palm to slow her down. 'Give it a little time.'

'Oh sod off, I'm not eighteen and playing hard to get,' she laughed.

'No, I know that, but have a *think* first. That's all I'm saying.'

'Yeah okay, you're right,' she said, taking another deep breath, then she turned away and started writing, her fingers like lightning on the keyboard.

Hi Amy, thank you. We had such a lovely time too. I've been really worried I'd put you off? I really enjoyed our walk. We'd like to get to know you both better and see where things go? Spa day sounds great. See you at 9 am? No pressure either. Em XxxX

Send.

Fuck.

*

CHAPTER FIVE

Emilia and Cassian arrived at the spa shortly before nine in the morning. The ride over had been beautiful, and as they had driven out of the city and into the countryside they had been treated to stunning views of the sun shining down through staggeringly large mountainous clouds onto a shroud of mist that had settled in lake-like pockets throughout the valley in which the spa was nestled.

Now they were pulling into the car park and coming to a stop as Cassian chuckled to himself again at how out of place their old Fiesta was amongst the Mercs, Beamers and Jags that had already arrived this morning.

The Aurora Spa & Country Club was set amongst several hundred acres of land and boasted a heated outdoor swimming pool, multiple jacuzzies and several private hot tubs. It also featured massage and aromatherapy sessions, Tai Chi, yoga, and a number of other group exercise and fitness classes. It was a membership only club and the fees were outlandish, but prospective members could pay for a single trial day, which plenty of people took advantage of. Even so, it was at the upper end of extravagant.

Emilia took her husband's hand as they walked towards the entrance and tried her best not to skip. After much deliberation, she had chosen a simple skirt and a sheer, loose white blouse, over a dark lace chemise. As they had been about to leave, however, she'd become self-conscious and had thrown on an old purple cardigan her mother had knitted ten years ago for her. It didn't really match the rest of her outfit, but she didn't feel *quite* so exposed.

'Do you think they're here already?' she said.

'I don't know, there's a lot of cars here.'

'What do they drive?'

'It was hard to see the other night, but I think it was a Merc,' said Cassian. 'Silver?'

Emilia looked around but there were quite a few silver Mercs parked up here, so she stopped speculating.

'Em, listen,' said Cassian. 'Try not to be too forward today, they might be thinking about this, they might not be. Let's not scare them off again, let's just all have a nice day together. Okay?'

'Okay,' she said as she nodded and squeezed his hand. 'I will.'

The entrance foyer was like a grander version of an old English country pub, with exposed beams, hardwood flooring, and ornate lamps adorning the walls. Emilia approached the reception desk and found a perky young blonde girl, no older than twenty, smiling back at her with wide eyes.

'Have Amy and Mark Hamilton arrived yet? We're meeting them here for, erm… a day at your spa?' she faltered and grinned.

'I'm afraid I'm not able to give out guest information,

Chapter Five

Miss?'

'Mrs Black,' she said, blushing.

'But if you're happy for me to do so, I can let them know you're here, if and when they arrive?'

'That would be lovely, thank you.'

'If you wish to wait for your friends, you're welcome to take a seat in the foyer.'

She took Cassian's hand again, and they headed over to a seat by the fireplace that overlooked the heated outdoor pool. There were already a couple of people swimming in the fresh morning air, and the mist in the forest beyond hadn't quite lifted, the blue morning hue giving the whole scene an almost eerie feel. For a moment she pictured Annie the porcelain doll, creeping out of the forest and she shivered.

'What time is it?' she asked.

'Ten past.'

'Do you think they're just running late?'

'No, I think they've bailed on us.'

'What? *Why?*' she said wide-eyed.

'I'm *kidding* Em, they're just running a few minutes late. Give them a break.'

But after almost half an hour had passed by, Emilia was starting to get worried.

'I'll text her,' she said, but as she started to pull out her phone, the door opened and in walked Amy, and Emilia's heart skipped several beats.

Dressed in an ankle-length sheer dress, with a plunging neckline and thigh-high slits on either side on her lightly freckled thighs, she looked *breathtaking,* and Emilia's stomach nosedived as butterflies *surged* through her chest. Behind her walked Mark, dressed casually in khaki shorts and a loose woven white buttoned shirt, looking devilishly handsome as she *squashed* her thighs together.

She immediately felt overdressed and working quickly she

managed to slip off her cardigan and *shove* it into their bag before Amy turned around.

'Hi, Sam, I'm sorry we're running late, do you know if Mr and Mrs Black are here yet?' said Amy to the perky young receptionist.

'Amy?' said Emilia standing up, suddenly feeling shy. Cassian stood up beside her and placed in hand in the small of her back, reassuring her.

Then Amy blushed, turned and smiled broadly and *rushed* over to greet them, embracing Emilia tightly and so suddenly that she failed to return the hug, and before she knew it her new friend was pulling away to hug her husband. In the somewhat awkward aftermath, Mark reached for Emilia's hand and shook it gently and then more firmly for Cassian as the two men smiled at one another.

'I'm so pleased you could come,' said Amy. 'Again, I'm *so* sorry about the other night. I hope you can forgive me. I was asking *stupid* questions, and-'

'It's fine, honestly,' said Emilia.

'So... what would you like to do first?' said Amy.

Emilia looked over at Cassian, who shrugged. 'We've not been here before, so we're open to suggestions?'

'Okay, then we'll surprise you,' said Amy, sounding mischievous. 'Just follow me.'

'Sounds good,' said Emilia, beaming at her as she glowed.

Amy stretched out her hand for her, and she took it with delight, noticing how soft her fingers were as they walked away from the men toward the sign for the pool, her whole body tingling with excitement.

Cassian watched as the girls chatted like old friends, walking along hand in hand, and for a moment he stood gazing at them, unsure what to do and feeling a little left out. Then Mark slapped him on the back and squeezed his shoulder.

Chapter Five

'Come on, mate. I'll show you where the changing rooms are,' he said, and winked. 'Did you bring your speedos?'

He laughed and snapped out of his gaze. 'The *tightest* I could find, mate.'

*

The pool itself turned out to be heated and as Cassian approached, he could feel the warmth emanating from a few feet away, the surface layered with a thin cloud of mist and steam. He had arrived poolside first and breathed in deeply in the cold morning air, finding it invigorating - it reminded him of sea swimming, back when he was studying down on the coast.

He and Emilia would wake up at five o'clock on Saturdays and head down to the beach to watch the sunrise, and then they would swim out to the marker buoy a little over a kilometre out to sea - the winner waiting for the loser, a kiss as the prize - and then swim back together side by side to shore.

As he drifted back to the present he could hear Mark walking up behind him and he turned to greet him, and laughed.

The man's appearance was *chiselled*. He looked like the model sculptors used in the Twelfth Century to accurately carve body parts for stone statues. Cassian's own physique was sharp, but Mark's was high definition.

The ex-soldier knelt down by the side of the pool and tested the water temperature, and then scooped up a handful, splashing it over his face and hair. 'Feels great to be out swimming this early at this time of year doesn't it?'

Cassian nodded.

'So you and Em?' he continued. 'You met at school?' he asked, turning back towards him as he nodded again.

'She was two years below me, she won't tell it like this, but she *relentlessly* pursued me.'

Mark stood up, listening as he grinned. 'She pursued you?'

'Like a *hound*, I was in my final year, with this pretty little lower school girl hanging around me at break and lunchtimes like a groupie. It was nice, she was sweet. One thing led to another and here we are.'

'Wait, one thing led to another?' said Mark. 'That's the worst storytelling gimmick. Imagine Romeo & Juliet like that? Romeo falls madly in love with Juliet at the Capulet ball, one thing leads to another and Juliet stabs herself in the chest because she can't live without her suicidal boyfriend?'

Cassian burst into laughter, shaking his head as Mark grinned. At the same time, Amy and Emilia came out of the changing rooms and stepped onto the path leading to the pool.

'What are you two giggling about?' said Amy as she drew near.

Cassian looked over at Mark. 'Nothing important.'

'Oh *no*, they're already best friends, the *bromance* has begun,' Amy stopped and tiptoed up to kiss her husband, and then she slipped on by and headed over to the steps.

Cassian couldn't help watching her walk away, her curves moving gently from side to side in her simple two-piece. She moved with a purpose, exuding confidence and charm, like a petite version of a pin-up girl from the fifties, and he could feel his chest tightening with every breath she stole.

Emilia had chosen a more conservative one-piece swimming costume with just a keyhole cut out on the small of her back, and *she* was feeling mightily intimidated.

Amy had a grace and beauty that only ever seemed reserved for celebrities, as though she was a classical film actress from a parallel universe where she had failed a few auditions, given up on acting and became an obscure artist

Chapter Five

instead.

She tried to settle her own mind by repeating her mantra that attractiveness is subjective, that Cassian saw her the way she saw Amy, but she did wonder if there was some truth to universal beauty. Helen of Troy was known as the face that launched a thousand ships. Perhaps one day Amy would be known as the face that mopped a thousand shits.

She started laughing to herself, and the other three all looked over, confused. 'Sorry, I just thought of something funny. Don't mind me.'

'Maybe one day you can tell me the joke,' said Amy, winking before she dived into the pool like a swan.

The water barely rippled.

Emilia followed, sitting down on the edge and lowering herself in, the surface feeling warm and cosy against her skin.

Cassian climbed down the nearby steps and pushed away from the edge, whilst Mark jumped in as though he was a living action movie cliché.

Amy resurfaced at the far end, her red hair now a dark shade of auburn, slicked back against her head as her freckles seemed to sparkle in the rising steam.

Emilia *yearned* to touch her, thinking back to their fleeting kiss, and she felt herself getting aroused, taking a shuddering breath as she hid her blush in the ripples. Beneath the water's edge, she subtly pressed her fingers into her crotch, squeezing her thighs together to quell the rising swell inside of her, and then with a deep breath, she swam forward into a gentle paddle, heading slowly towards the far end.

On arrival she swam up next to Amy, briefly dunking her head, before resurfacing facing down the pool, both of them treading water, their fingers occasionally touching beneath the surface, then she smiled and pushed away from the edge and settled into a gentle breaststroke, as her heart *thumped*.

* * *

*

After swimming for another half an hour, both couples left the pool and headed over to the jacuzzi, which was situated in a small and secluded clearing a few metres into the forest that surrounded the spa. As the others had watched, mesmerised, Amy had run along the path in front of them and climbed the short steps, slipping down into the warm water and submersing herself completely. Mark, ever the gentlemen, had helped Emilia up onto the side, and then walked around to the controls, turning up the heat and setting the jets to medium. There had followed a low rumble and Amy had sat up, startled as a bubble of jets had shot up from underneath her.

'*Oh*,' she said, raising her eyebrows, and then holding out her hand to steady Emilia's descent into the water.

A few seconds later, both the men vaulted the edge and slid down onto the circular ridge of seating under the surface, stretching out their arms and relaxing as Amy settled back and placed the palm of her hand tentatively on Emilia's thigh.

A series of thoughts rapidly began racing through her mind as her skin-tingled and her muscles froze. Should she touch Amy's hand *too?* Should she touch her thigh? Should she do *nothing?* What was Amy *doing?* Now she was *squeezing* her thigh softly amongst the jets of bubbles and Emilia couldn't help but think of the Duchess and Lady Victoria underneath the blanket, the roaring fire - the Duke.

Fuck it.

She decided to stop thinking and just act, and as her chest thumped, she slipped her fingers over the top of Amy's and intertwined them gently, and as she felt the heat of her skin through the water, her chest filled with butterflies, heart filled with desire, and her warmth *throbbed*.

Chapter Five

'Have you ever had sex in a jacuzzi?' said Amy, suddenly as then she looked over at Emilia. 'And don't say, *No, would you like to?* I know what you're like.'

Emilia laughed nervously, conflicted as Amy rubbed her thigh sweetly under the water.

'We did, actually. A few years ago in the Swiss Alps,' said Cassian.

'No way,' gasped Amy.

'Nice,' said Mark. 'Holiday?'

Cassian nodded. 'Incredible place, the views are magnificent. We spent a whole day hiking around Oeschinensee, and another paddling about on the lake.'

'I climbed the Matterhorn, around six years ago,' said Mark.

'Of course you did,' laughed Amy. 'Naked and carrying a machine gun whilst rescuing orphaned puppies, probably.'

Cassian laughed as Mark smiled. 'It's a beautiful country,' he said.

'The place we stayed has a *slide* down the side of the mountain,' said Cassian.

Amy's eyes widened as she sat forward. 'Oh *wow*. We have *got* to go there.'

At the same time, Emilia moved her arm down from the side of the pool, and pressed her palm against Amy's spine, just above her bottom. It might have been her imagination, but as her friend leant back, it felt as though she was nuzzling herself onto her.

'You must have travelled a lot in the army?' said Cassian.

Mark nodded. 'To some of the best places, and most of the worst ones.'

'Why did you leave?'

'After my enlistment contract ended, I got offered better a job that paid more and carried less risk.'

'Protection work?'

'That's right,' he nodded, stretching out.

Amy leaned closer to Emilia and squeezed her hand under the water. 'Shall we leave them to it, Em? Go relax in the steam room?' she said, standing up. 'They can have their boy talk then, and we can have… a little girl talk?'

'Okay, sure,' said Emilia, suddenly feeling anxious about the idea of spending time alone with Amy. All the while they'd been together in the pool and the jacuzzi, she hadn't felt the need to *talk* about the last time they'd met, and their kiss. But the idea of being alone with her again was incredibly exciting too.

Amy reached out her hand and she stood up, water cascading off her hips as she followed the graceful freckled figure out of the bubbling jacuzzi.

'See you for lunch,' Emilia said to her husband as she passed him, dripping wet and more than a little aroused as she followed Amy down the tree-lined path to the changing rooms. They walked past the pool holding hands and her new friend held the door open for her as they headed back through.

In the privacy of the changing area, the gorgeous redhead pulled off her bikini bottoms, momentarily exposing her behind, followed by her top, allowing Emilia to catch a glimpse of the side of her breast, and then she wrapped herself in a small white towel before handing another to Emilia, who was a little more reserved but did the same as Amy turned around.

Towels secured and wrapped tightly around them both, Amy led the way.

On the outside, the sauna was fairly basic, with white plastic windows and a PVC door that looked much the same as most backdoors in kitchens across the country, but inside it was *luxurious*, with fine wood seating that Emilia found to be comfortable and smooth.

Chapter Five

Amy stepped inside and shuffled up to the far end, loosening her towel slightly and then beckoning for Emilia to join her. She smiled and closed her eyes as her new friend sat down to the left and slightly across from her and for a little while, they sat in silence, enjoying the warmth of the room, the sweat building on their skin, feeling their pores opening up, and breathing in the steam deeply. Emilia was just starting to relax when the silence was broken.

'I'm sorry I ran away,' said Amy, abruptly.

Emilia looked over at her but didn't say anything.

'I got scared,' she continued. She took a deep breath, drawing the steam deep into her lungs. 'I like you, and I got scared because I want to be friends with you,' she paused, opened her eyes and looked over at Emilia. 'I'm sorry.'

'It's okay,' she said, but her heart was already aching and the little crack that had begun to heal, burst wide open again. She had gotten her hopes up, and now Amy was bringing her crashing back down again.

'No. It's not, okay,' said Amy, her voice cracking. 'Because I *kissed* you and it was a really, *really* good kiss, and it wasn't fair, and I can't stop thinking about it.' Emilia frowned and then laughed as Amy closed her eyes again. 'And I keep *touching* you, and you keep touching me, and it's driving me fucking *wild*. I can't stop thinking about you, and when I'm with you, my mind is just racing and thinking about how I can touch you again, or hoping you might touch me, so I can feel that feelin-'

Emilia leant across suddenly, interrupting her friend's diatribe, and cupped her cheek in the palm of her hand, and then *kissed* her softly on the lips.

And the world turned.

She took it slow, kissing her soft and deep, tracing her thumb across the top of the redhead's ear as their lips pecked sweetly at each other.

It was *delicate* and soft, and she tasted sweet and wet.

After a while, she began to pull away but Amy pulled her *back* with both hands, kissing her lips again and again, and as she did so, Emilia put her knee down on the wood beside her thigh, and then ran her hand down the girl's shoulder, playing with the edge of the towel wrapped tightly around her, just above her breasts. They stopped kissing for a moment, just holding each other, breathing hard and looking into each other eyes as their heart's pounded.

'If we were to do this,' whispered Amy, her voice barely more than a breath. 'How would it work?'

'What do you mean?' said Emilia, her whole body quivering with desire.

'If we were to all… you *know*,' Amy squeezed her hips. 'How would it work?'

Emilia's stomach flipped and she felt a powerful wave of anxiety run through her like a jolt of electricity. She wasn't even sure she'd *heard* Amy correctly, as though the steam might have blocked her ears. 'I don't know,' she said, her eyes wide.

'You must have thought about it.'

'A *little* bit,' said Emilia, as she fought the urge to clamp her thighs down tight.

Amy raised her eyebrows as if to say *only a little?*

'Okay, yes. A *lot*,' laughed Emilia, gasping. 'But what do you want me to do, draw you a diagram?'

'No, but also *yes* I would, and we'll come back to that later,' she nodded. 'What I mean to say is… would we… *make love?* Would Cassian and I? You and Mark? *What do you want?*'

'What do *we* want?' asked Emilia, barely able to contain herself now, her whole body bursting with desperation.

The girls sat in silence, bristling with nervous energy and tension until Amy spoke at last. 'For it to be nice,' she said.

Chapter Five

Emilia smiled. She desperately wanted to kiss her again, but she didn't want to scare her away. Instead, she said. 'So do I,' very quietly.

'I need to talk to Mark,' said Amy, breathing deep. 'I mean we've talked about it already, but I can't just spring this on him. We need to talk about it *properly*.'

'Take as long as you need,' gushed Emilia. 'I don't want to rush this.'

But her heart was already *racing*.

*

After leaving the steam room, Amy and Emilia had showered and dressed and returned to the main bar area, where they found the men drinking coffee and chatting animatedly.

As the girls approached, Cassian called for the waiter, ordering two more cups of coffee and a menu for lunch, and a short while later they ate together, laughing and smiling. Even Emilia managed to stay calm and relaxed, with only the occasional shakes, heart palpitations and moments of sheer panic.

Afterwards, Amy suggested that they all had couples massages and after booking themselves in, Emilia and Cassian waited until their allotted time before heading in, disrobing again, and relaxing under the strong yet tender hands of two professional masseurs.

As their bodies unwound and released the tension of the past few weeks, Emilia stretched out her hand to Cassian, who was laying on the bed next to hers, and they held hands as she mouthed *I love you*, to him and smiled.

Refreshed, relaxed and renewed they collected their clothes again, dressed, and headed out into the main foyer, ready to head home after an incredible and exciting day. Emilia felt more than ever, that this was the right thing to do, but in the foyer stood Amy and Mark, both looking more nervous than usual - as though something was *wrong*.

Emilia's heart felt heavy as she walked across towards them, hand in hand with Cassian, and all of a sudden she felt a sharp pang of guilt that she hadn't spoken to him about what Amy had said earlier in the sauna, but it was too late now. Amy's face was nervous, and she was licking and chewing her lip as they drew closer.

Even Cassian began to frown. 'What's wrong?' he said as they approached.

Amy looked at them both, and then back at Mark who nodded.

'Erm, would you guys like to stay the night?' said Amy. 'Here?'

Emilia's heart *lurched* as the butterflies in her tummy all took flight at once. 'Oh. *Yes*,' she said, barely hesitating. 'I mean, erm. Cass? Would you like to stay?'

He looked across at her, wide-eyed and startled, and saw her flash a brief and happy smile. 'Sure, why not?'

Fuck, he's good, she thought as she admired his cool response.

'Fantastic,' said Amy, her body alive with a crackling energy. 'We could see if we can get adjoining rooms and then have a nightcap? What do you think, Mark?'

'Sounds great,' he said, grinning wildly as he winked at Cassian. 'I'll go get the room keys. Then we can have dinner and head up. Cass, do you want to come with me and grab a bottle from the bar for later?'

'Sure,' he said, turning and frowning at his wife. 'See you in a bit?'

Amy looked over at her as their husbands disappeared toward the bar, and for the first time since they had met, Emilia thought that the confident, unshakeable and exuberant redhead, looked a little vulnerable.

Chapter Five

'Is this okay?' said Amy. 'Staying, I mean? You didn't seem sure. I sort of thought you-'

Emilia reached her hand out and took Amy's, who looked a little startled at the gesture. '*Yes*. I want to stay. Is this what you want too?' she glanced down at their hands, both shaking.

Amy started to blush. She closed her eyes and tried to stay calm and measured, but she looked for a moment like she was going to burst into tears. 'I think so. We talked about it,' she said, her voice had gone quiet and soft. 'Mark is okay with us… you know. In fact, he's quite *enthusiastic*, I think he rather fancies you, but I'm not sure if I'm-'

'Ready?' she finished.

'Yes,' she said, smiling and relaxing a little.

Emilia could see her eyes had glazed over with a sheen of tears. 'I'm not sure we are either, but we don't have to rush anything,' she reached out and stroked her fingers. 'I really like you. *We* really like you both.'

Amy smiled and scrunched her eyes then took a deep breath, exhaling hard as she bristled with nervous energy. 'Where are those *men?*'

A few minutes later they were all settling down to dinner in the main restaurant, during which Amy spent most of the meal mercilessly teasing Emilia with her toes. Now, a couple of hours later they were making their way up the stairs to the third floor of the building, laughing and flirting and full of excitement.

It was quiet on the landing, a few towels sat in heaps outside doors, waiting to be collected and a small cleaning cart abandoned at the far end. Wall sconces illuminated the door numbers and Amy led Emilia by the hand excitedly, with the two men following behind, stopping when she reached the first room.

She pressed the key card against the handle and there was

a gentle beep, then the door unlatched and she swung it open effortlessly with the palm of her hand. Inside, the room began to light up. Spotlights underneath the bed illuminating the thick pile carpet, the sleek embedded illuminations slowly brightening in sequence.

'Here's your card,' said Amy, handing it over to Emilia, her hand shaking, bobbing up and down as she spoke. 'Shall we meet back here in ten minutes? You can knock on the adjoining door?'

'Sure,' said Emilia as she grabbed Cassian by his shirt and pulled him towards their room. She fumbled with their card, dropping it onto the floor, and her husband picked it up and placed it back between her quivering fingers as she turned around before pressing it hard against the reader, heading inside.

'Oh *shit*,' she said, leaning against the wood as it shut behind her. 'Is this really happening?'

'I guess so?'

'Is this okay?'

Cassian approached and placed his hands on either side of her face, stroking her cheeks and eyebrows with his thumbs, something he would often do to calm her down.

'Yes,' he said. 'Is there anything you want to talk about?'

'Like what?'

'Things you don't feel comfortable with.'

Emilia turned away and sat down on the bed. 'I guess so, but I don't think it's going to be like that. I just want to see where things go. I want it to be nice and so does Amy. I *trust* them.'

He sat down next to her and put his arm over her shoulder as she hugged him tight and kissed him, then pulled away.

'We should probably get ready,' she laughed. 'Should I perfume my knickers?'

'I love you,' he grinned, looking at her serenely. There

Chapter Five

followed a long and happy silence as they gazed into each other's eyes, and then Emilia leaned forward.

'I love you too,' she said, melting.

*

CHAPTER SIX

Emilia knocked tentatively on the adjoining door as she waited, a bottle of wine in her shaking hand. She tried to be patient, but she was bristling with excitement and barely able to stand still, hopping from one foot to the other.

A moment later Amy opened it a crack and peered around the edge. 'Yes? Can I help you?'

'Police, we're looking for a couple? One's a shit artist and the other one looks like a statue that's escaped from Ancient Rome?'

Amy's serious face crumbled and she burst into laughter and opened the door wide, revealing that she had changed into a black lace bodycon dress, and Emilia found herself struggling not to stare.

'You've found us, officer. Bang to rights,' she turned away as she took the wine from Emilia's hands, passing it to Mark who opened it with one twist. 'We've only got a single set of wine glasses,' continued Amy. 'So maybe grab yours?'

Chapter Six

Cassian produced their pair from behind his back and set them down on the side table. As he did, Mark walked over and poured out four equal glasses, and then picked up the first two and handed them to Emilia and Cassian, before passing another to his wife who had taken a perch on the edge of the *enormous* bed.

She looked up at Emilia and patted the duvet beside her and said. 'Come, sit with me.'

Cassian sat down on one of the two armchairs that faced the bed and Mark put down his glass and settled into the other one, facing the two girls as each man took a long, deep breath.

'So... what do you think of the spa?' said Amy, awkwardly.

'It's *nice*,' said Emilia, quietly.

There was an uncomfortably long silence as the foursome sipped their wine, broken finally when Amy spoke.

'Oh *shit*, I'm so nervous,' she laughed and then she covered her mouth, biting her lip as Emilia looked across at her, blushing as the silence returned.

And there they met each other's gaze and *held* it.

After a deep breath, Amy wriggled across and raised her hand up to run her fingers through a loose slip of Emilia's hair, then she shuffled closer again until their thighs touched, hesitatingly briefly, before leaning in to kiss her, and as their lips met, her warm hand traced the contour of Emilia's cheek and neck.

This is happening, thought Emilia. *We're really going to do this.*

Then she realised with a surge of arousal, excitement and guilt that for the first time in their lives, she was *kissing* someone else in front of Cassian.

She felt her heart flutter and surge at the sensation of Amy's other hand moving slowly up her waist. Then she turned, working herself further up onto the bed and running her own hand through the girl's fiery red hair.

Amy's wandering hand reached Emilia's breast and she felt herself rise off the bed at her touch, leaning into her and kissing her harder. She stopped and took a deep shuddering breath, turning to look over towards Cassian and Mark, both men sitting in their armchairs, smiling, watching and enjoying the show.

Amy looked over too and then beckoned to them, returning immediately and urgently to Emilia's soft and beautiful lips. Quivering, she ran her hands down her new friend's legs, finding the hem of her lace dress, and then she began to slide it up the outside of her thigh, letting her short nails lightly scratch her pale skin as she did so, and making her breathe in sharply. Then she squeezed the top of her leg, feeling her hip bone beneath and moved her hand around to her bottom, searching for the edge of her underwear.

Amy let out a soft breath as Emilia's fingers found purchase, and then she let out an even louder one as she felt Mark kneel onto the bed beside her and kiss her neck deeply.

Emilia sensed Cassian next to her now too, his strong hands stroking her back and caressing her shoulders, and then he was pulling her blouse off and over her head as Amy pulled away and turned her head to kiss her own husband deeply on the lips. At the same time, Cassian was kissing Emilia's ears and neck, working his hands down her shoulders and pulling the strap of her chemise down so it fell loose onto her arm.

It was all happening so fast it was rapidly becoming *overwhelming*.

Amy turned back and was facing her again, Mark kneeling over his wife's shoulder, looking down at Emilia's breasts inside her top, loose and open, her nipple on show to them both and suddenly she felt self-conscious.

Chapter Six

This was *really* happening.

They were all going to make love together.

It was all so *intense*.

She began to panic, but then Amy was kneeling up on the bed and wrapping her arms around her head, pressing her face into her breasts and kissing her sweety as she covered her up, and then she heard a whisper in her ear. 'Are you okay?' she said, and somehow she felt relaxed again. Her words had *soothed* her.

This was safe, this was right.

She nodded imperceptibly, and then Amy took her hand and placed it back against her bottom and Emilia *squeezed* and laughed and then pulled back, turning to kiss Cassian.

'I love you, you know that don't you?' she said as she pulled away from his lips.

He nodded as she started to unbutton his shirt, one by one and then she looked over at Amy who began to do the same to Mark who was kissing Amy's neck as she worked on him, unable to keep his hands off her.

For a brief second, Emilia thought about how much she wanted Mark's hands on her too, and then Cassian was kissing her again and holding her face in his palms and she melted. She could *feel* how aroused he was, his member *throbbing* in his jeans, and quickly she began to undo his belt as he knelt up on the bed, loosening the clasp and sliding the strap out of the buckle and then unzipping his fly and shimmying them down toward his knees.

Pausing, she looked over toward Mark and Amy and found them watching, Amy facing them as Mark's hand delicately circled her crotch through her lacy dress. She had one hand up and around his neck and the other was stroking the bulge in his shorts, and she smiled at Emilia before turning her gaze back toward Cassian's swelling underwear.

Emilia took her cue and looked up at her husband as she

dipped the front of his boxers down and then with a slow reverence, she reached inside for his rock hard cock.

Closing her hand around it, she found him to be harder than *ever*, and with a skin-tingling giddiness, she slowly teased it back up and out, sliding her palm up and down the shaft, feeling him dripping with excitement. Then she watched as he turned to look at Amy, and felt him twinge against her fingers as he did so.

Suddenly her new friend was moving across the bed, dropping onto all fours and sliding past her and before Emilia knew what was happening, Cassian's cock was *inside* her mouth and her husband was looking up at her, shocked and almost *pleading*, but then he closed his eyes and his mouth dropped open as she worked her way up and down him, and he started to bend forward as she pulled his boxers down completely.

Emilia saw that Mark was looking on, almost as shocked as Cassian, but she could see that he was *happy* - he wasn't upset or jealous - in fact, he was even *more* excited than before.

She looked back down and then reached to move Amy's hair aside so she could see better, and then she stretched up to reach Cassian's face and kissed him long and slow, feeling the gentle rhythmic sensation below her of Amy *sucking* his cock.

Cassian was beginning to look desperate and Amy could sense that he was getting close too fast, so she slowed down and pulled back and kissed the tip of his glans softly with her cherry red lips, making him twitch and nearly lose control. Then she sat back up on her knees, smiling at him with wide and happy eyes, before flicking her guilty gaze between the other two.

Mark knelt forward now and placed his hands around the edge of Amy's dress and went to pull it up and over her head, but Emilia reached out and stopped him, shaking her

Chapter Six

head and smiling mischievously.

Instead, she raised Amy's arms up in the air first and then slowly rolled the dress up with Mark's help, kissing first her bare stomach, and then her proud ribs, and then her chest and the valley between her breasts, and then finally her neck and lips - on which she could *taste* her husband - before the dress finally came away, leaving her in just her knickers and bra.

Mark stood up a moment later and removed his shirt, a few items of clothing behind the others, as Amy turned and helped him out of his khakis and then he was back on the bed, and she was pushing him down so he was lying flat.

Now she took hold of Emilia's hand and guided her over to where her husband lay and started teasing her fingers over the material of his underwear, his rock hard cock pointing straight up, and with a sudden twitch, it *popped* through the gap and Emilia could see it at last.

She paled and grinned, unconsciously licking her lips as her whole body quivered with taboo desire. It was slightly smaller than Cassian's but *thicker* somehow, and it had a slight bend to it, curving upwards. She reached out hesitantly and touched it with the tips of her fingers as she glanced sideways at Amy for reassurance.

Behind her she felt Cassian moving to see what she was doing, then she felt his warm and comforting hand touching the small of her back. He kissed her neck and then turned to Amy who slipped her arms around his shoulder, and then he kissed *her* softly on the lips too.

Emilia continued to stroke Mark as she watched Cassian unhook Amy's bra and slide it off over her shoulder and arms, then without any hesitation he lay her down and pulled off her knickers, and Emilia *thrilled* at the sight of Amy's naked body as she knelt up and sat before them.

Unabashed, her eyes glided over her; her sweet freckles,

spread like an eagle across her chest, her sweet little curves, her handful breasts and her small delicate nipples, and then her hips, and between, her sweet little slit, bare and glistening.

Cassian moved behind Amy now, his cock pressing against her ass, and as Emilia turned her attention back to Mark, she could see in the corner of her eye that he was kissing her neck, his arm tight around her waist, his hand on her flat and pale stomach. Slowly, she leaned down so her lips were just an inch above Mark's tip, and then as she plucked up the courage, she took him into her, and the whole world spun.

He felt *huge* in her mouth.

She swirled her tongue around his head tentatively and felt as his warmth leaked into her cheeks, and somehow she felt him *grow* inside of her if that were even possible. Then feeling guilty, she slipped him out and turned to see Amy stroking Cassian's cock as they both watched her sucking Mark.

She could *feel* the excitement in her chest - the sensation of another man having been in her *mouth* was overwhelming and she tried not to think about the possibility of him pushing it *inside* her, perhaps later. Then she took him back between her lips again and slid him up and down.

As Mark began to moan hard, she sat back and Amy embraced her, lips on lips, tongue on tongue, and as they kissed she felt their men moving on the bed, and now someone was behind her and they were removing her skirt, sliding it down over her bottom and then someone *else* was pulling her chemise off, finally exposing her breasts, and then she was almost naked and pressed up against Amy's bare body.

The feeling was *incredible*.

Her soft skin was smooth and electrifying, her red hair vibrant and loose, flowing gently over her supple frame, and as they embraced she felt prickles all over her body, as

Chapter Six

though goosebumps had erupted across all of her skin, but most of all she felt *warm* and cosy.

The pair of them fell forward and wrapped their arms and legs around each other, kissing one another urgently, stroking and caressing, curling and squeezing, and then Amy's fingers were between her thighs, urgently pulling her wet knickers down to her knees, searching up and finding her naked lips, then sliding up and down between them.

Oh, yes.

Emilia felt a deep urge to *squeeze* her new friend, to hold her as tightly as she could, to smell her hair and nuzzle into her neck, to kiss her cheeks and her forehead and her lips over and over. The warmth and softness of her skin was intoxicating and her head tingled as though she was floating through a cloud. And then Amy's fingers started exploring her *delicately*, and then slowly and carefully, she slipped a single fingertip inside her and pushed.

Emilia let out a gasp and squeezed her thighs together, but then she felt Cassian - or Mark - pushing her knees apart and Amy was rolling her to the side. Now on her back, with her eyes closed, she felt Amy start to *kiss* her way past and down her neck, across her collarbone and then around her breast, teasing and touching her.

Then she felt a wave of pleasure as Amy's lips found her nipple, and for a few quiet moments, the whole world faded away. But then she was moving *further* down, and her friend's weight shifted. Now she was kissing her stomach, and then her belly button, making her quiver and writhe on the bed, arching her spine.

Now her waist.

Her hips.

Her *mound*.

Emilia bit her lip as she felt Amy's hot breath between her thighs, and she gripped the duvet and buried her head to one side, and then let out a long *slow* moan as her friend's tongue ran its way along the length of her warmth, and began to slowly circle her clit.

'*Yes,*' she whispered as her mouth opened wide.

She lowered her hands and found soft red hair, running her fingers through it in ecstasy as Amy's tongue flicked and pressed and slipped against her. Now she could feel two slender and long fingers inside her and she let out a whimper, louder this time, as she pressed upwards and kept *swirling* her tongue at the same perfect rate.

'*Yes,*' said cried again as she started to feel something powerful building inside of her.

She could feel the bed shifting and she opened her eyes to find Cassian kneeling next to her, his cock inches from her mouth. Without hesitating she took him in, sliding him over her tongue, tasting him as Amy kept going, her fingers moving, pulsing, *tapping*, deep inside her pussy.

She felt a new sensation now, a rhythmic movement and looked down to see that Mark was behind Amy. She smiled as they made eye contact and he then tilted his head backwards, holding onto his wife's ass. Then Amy *moaned* into her crotch as he pushed his cock deep inside her and began to fuck his wife.

Within seconds Emilia was close and she took Cassian back into her mouth again as her orgasm built, but it quickly became too much. He slid out as she began to moan and her legs pinched together, then she arched her back, her skin tingling with love, her fingers stretched out, her mouth wide… and then she *shook* as her whole body came.

For a few blissful moments, she lay there in euphoric harmony, feeling the bed moving back and forth as Mark made love to the woman between her thighs, feeling Cassian's warm hand in her own, squeezing her, comforting her and keeping her safe.

Chapter Six

She had never felt like this before - so wanted, so *loved*. It was *wonderful*.

Now Amy was moving. She had pulled away from Mark and was turning over to lay on her back and now he was thrusting between his wife's legs and pushing back inside her, fucking her hard and holding her face as he kissed her passionately.

'Harder,' she said and then she turned to look back at Emilia and reached out for her hand, her fingers searching and desperate as they interlocked.

Cassian knelt between Emilia's legs now, and as she stared into Amy's eyes, she felt her husband's wet cock pushing and probing and then *sliding* into her *soaking* wet pussy, and she squeezed her friend's fingers and smiled as they made love beside one another.

It was happening.

The moment she'd fantasised about.

It was happening now and *all around her*.

She watched closely as Amy's eyes began to glaze over, her lips parting, wider and wider as she got closer and closer to the edge. Now she was beginning to arch her back, to dig her fingers into Mark's back muscles, and then she started to moan, louder and *louder* with each thrust.

'Yes, *harder*,' she commanded as Mark quickened his pace.

Her face started to flush and her hand crushed Emilia's fingers and then suddenly, she was coming again *too* and together they climaxed, just *seconds* apart. Squeezing each other, holding each other, *stroking* each other.

It was perfect.

It was *everything* she had wanted.

Her body *glowed*.

But neither of the men were done.

They both watched calmly as their wives recovered - their breathing returning to normal, their heart rates slowing. The girls holding each other's hands, their heads close together on the pillow, Emilia stroking Amy's face as Cassian spooned next to her. Mark on the other side of Amy, holding her tight in his big strong arms.

After a while Emilia rolled over and kissed Cassian hard on the lips, holding his face in her hands. Then she looked into his eyes, questioning and sweet.

'Would it… be okay?' she said, her voice full of unspoken meaning.

Cassian returned her gaze with kind eyes, and then he looked over at Mark, and finally back at his wife. 'Yes,' he said. 'If it's okay with them?'

Emilia rolled over and took Amy's hands again. 'Would you like to?' she asked.

Amy blinked and in that moment, just as she had seen it before downstairs in the foyer, she looked *vulnerable* again. For a long few seconds, she stared warmly into Emilia's eyes, considering, and then she nodded quickly.

Instantly Emilia leaned into her and kissed her hard, but this time she rolled up and on top of her, laughing and giggling as she did so, tickling and pressing their breasts together and entwining their fingers, and then she was rolling over the top and down the other side.

At the same time, Amy shifted over towards Cassian and then smiled a mischievous smile at him, and instead of laying back, she rolled onto her *front*, raising her bottom up, just a little, and sliding her legs and thighs apart.

Emilia looked wide-eyed at the pair of them and then turned her head to look at Mark who grinned and placed a gentle, reassuring hand upon her stomach. Then he gestured with his eyes for her to watch, and she rolled onto her side again, her ass nestled against Mark's proud cock as she blushed.

For a brief and exhilarating moment, she felt it twitch

against her, so she reached down behind her back and took it in her hand, playing with it softly as she grinned, and then she focused her attention on her own husband, and Amy.

Cassian looked to her as if to check for permission one last time, and she smiled in response and nodded. Then she felt Mark's hand sliding down her stomach as he shifted down the bed, his cock in her hand, sliding against her ass as she moved it to rest between the back of her thighs.

Now Cassian was lining himself up behind Amy, and Amy was tilting her ass up higher towards his hard cock, her palms flat on the bed, her elbows up, her dark red hair falling over her cheek. Cass's hands came down either side of her next, his face close enough to smell her hair, and Emilia watched her pale beautiful face as his cock lined up, thick and hard, and then slid gently and smoothly inside of her.

Amy's eyes closed and she *flushed* and shook, and after a few blissful seconds, she let out a gentle whimper of pure pleasure.

Emilia felt Mark's cock surge and grow between her fingers and she quickened her pace sliding up and down his shaft, squeezing him softly, reassuring him, and teasing him against her wet pussy, and then his strong hands were turning her onto her front and his knees came down between her legs, and before she could even gasp, she was being pulled up by her hips onto all fours.

A heartbeat later she felt the head of his cock pressing against her urgently, and then her mind *whirled* as she felt herself opening up as he pushed himself forward, and slipped into her for the very first time.

Yes.

Mark was inside her, not Cassian.

For the first time in her *life*, there was another man's cock inside her pussy, and it felt so incredibly *good*.

She looked to her right and saw both Cass and Amy

watching them, smiling and slowly making love, her husband's eyes opening and closing, alternating between watching her with Mark and feeling the intense pleasure of Amy's fresh pussy.

Mark's manhood felt taboo and new, and her whole body tingled with illicit pleasure. This was so wrong, and yet it was clearly so *right*.

He was *thick*. Thicker than Cass, and she could feel herself being stretched more than usual as he took her. She could feel him growing and pulsing inside of her with each thrust, and it felt mind-blowing and exhilarating.

She sensed him turn his head behind her looking over at Cassian and Amy, watching as her husband pushed down gently into his wife, listening to her *moan*, watching her grip the bedsheets in her fingers, and in that moment she felt the most incredible sense of comfort and love.

He looked down at Emilia, at her beautiful body, her shape, the way she moved, the way she *fucked*, the way she *sounded*. She felt wonderful too, her pussy tight and warm, and he could feel himself building to climax already.

He listened to his wife and knew that she was getting close, and Cassian too, he thought. The man's pace was changing, and he was pushing harder and Amy was moaning *louder* with every thrust.

Emilia could feel Mark building inside her too, and she started to panic.

He was going to come inside her.

No one but Cass had *ever* come inside her before, and now here she was, in a spa hotel, getting fucked by an ex-soldier whilst her own husband was shagging a *gorgeous* redhead that she might be in love with.

In love.

There it was. That was the truth of it. *She was in love*. The thought thrilled her.

Chapter Six

'Come inside me,' she whispered.

'Are you sure?' gasped Mark.

'*Uh-huh,*' she said, gripping the bedsheets, her eyes shut *tight* and her mouth wide open.

As Mark started to moan louder and louder, she looked over to Cassian who was gazing back at her, his eyes wide open as if asking for permission.

Amy's hand shot out from her side and fumbled for Emilia's and finding it they clasped their fingers together tight, then she looked back at Mark and *nodded* and Emilia caught Cassian's eye again and did the same, and then both men began to speed up and moan and spasm as they thrust.

Emilia watched as Cassian shuddered and orgasmed and a split second later, she knew that Amy could *feel* it, as she came too, her eyes rolling up into her head as a loud moan escaped her thin, sweet lips.

Then Emilia felt Mark *surge* inside of her and a split second later she felt him pulse and twitch, warmth spreading throughout her pussy, filling her up, and she moaned and buried her head into the pillow, squeezing Amy's hand so tight she cried out.

Yes.

Mark had finished inside her. Cassian had finished inside Amy. They had *all* come at once.

All of them together, in perfect *harmony*.

For some time after they lay still, not moving, just breathing and holding each other.

Mark was deep inside her still, and she could feel that he was hard, gently moving back and forth, after a while he slipped out of her and leaned forward to kiss her. Then she saw that Cassian and Amy were kissing too, and after a few more beautiful seconds, the men rolled aside and the girls faced each other, smiling.

'*Wow,*' laughed Amy, her smile unable to go any wider.

She leaned in and pressed her mouth against Emilia's, her kiss long and slow. This time, Amy rolled over the top of Emilia and ended up back in Mark's arms as Cassian shuffled towards his wife and embraced her.

For a while they all cuddled, Cassian stroking his wife's hair and kissing her, Mark doing the same with Amy, her head on his chest, his arm slung around her shoulders, their fingers interwoven.

'You know,' said Amy, interrupting the hazy bliss. 'I read this article a couple of days ago, that said men who engage in group sex have a reduced refractory period, and get hard again if there's another woman around to shag.'

Emilia rolled her head to look at Amy, bemused and frowning, and then she watched with increasing trepidation as she slipped off the bed and walked over to her bag which was still on the thickly carpeted floor. She unzipped it and produced a small bottle, then she turned and nimbly hopped back onto the bed.

'Lay down, on your front,' she said to Emilia.

Confused, she collected her hair in her hands and rolled away from Cassian to lay down, letting it fall on one side so she could see what was happening.

Their men shuffled down the bed to watch as Amy squirted a small amount of lube onto her fingers, then she looked up and smiled at them both.

Cassian's mouth dropped wide open a moment later, his eyes barely blinking as Amy knelt forward between Emilia's outstretched legs and with her dry hand, stroked her girl's curvy bottom - first her rump, and then the crease where her ass met her thigh. Then her fingers traced slowly down between her cheeks, all the way along from her spine.

Oh, gosh.

Gently, she pushed Emilia cheek's apart and exposed her, before she could process what was happening, there was another sensation, intense and overwhelming, and *surprising*, as Amy's finger teased her *asshole*.

Oh, fuck.

Emilia shuddered with pleasure as Amy started to coat her taboo little entrance with lube and she giggled and squirmed on the bed.

'It's cold,' she cried.

'Sorry,' laughed Amy, rubbing her hands together to warm them.

Now there was a different sensation. One of pressure as Amy teased her finger inside Emilia's sweet hole. She swirled it around gently at first, pushing and probing and then she pushed a little harder and it went inside easily.

For a few moments, Amy slipped her lubed digit in and out of her as she writhed and moaned on the bed gasping with delight as she tried to catch her breath, occasionally pausing and withdrawing to apply more of the slick liquid. Then with her free hand, Amy began to play with her clit too, warming her up.

Cassian was now practically beside himself, shaking and quivering, barely able to contain his excitement over what he was seeing.

Then suddenly, Amy leaned in close and Emilia felt her tongue lick all the way up from her clit, along her lips, past her pussy, over her perineum and across *there*, and she lost it.

She quivered and shook and cried out in ecstasy as Amy's tongue probed and pushed and *licked* her ass, and then as suddenly as she'd started, she *stopped*, leaving her a broken wreck, pulsing and jerking on the bed, fingers squeezing the sheets until her knuckles turned white.

After a few moments, she became aware that Amy was making Cassian lay down beside her and then she was being hauled onto her knees by Mark's strong arms.

Then Amy kissed her hard on the lips and stroked her hair

and said, 'How would you like to have one *here*, and one… *here*.'

Oh my goodness.

Could she even take both of them at once? she thought to herself. Then she nodded, *urgently*.

Amy wriggled aside and Emilia moved over, quickly straddling her own husband, placing her hands on either side of his chest and then lowering herself down onto his waiting, familiar cock, feeling it surge and tease and push up and into her. For a fleeting moment, she thought about Mark's seed, still warming her insides, and how it made Cassian's cock feel different and more slippery, and then her eyes met his and both of them gazed at one another, filled with love as their bodies reconnected.

For a few moments, she rode him, up and down, feeling his length and girth inside of her again, feeling *both* of them there. Then she slowed down and came to a stop, his cock firmly erect and throbbing.

Now she felt Mark behind her, felt his knees pushing into the mattress, his hands around her waist, stroking her back with his thumbs, positioning himself and lining up. Then Amy was in front of her, holding her face and smiling, straddling her thighs over Cassian's waiting mouth.

There followed a warm sensation against her ass as Mark poured more lube onto her and himself, and then she felt the tip of his slick cock probing and pressing against her hole, his hands on her ass, Cassian's cock twitching inside her pussy.

This was it.

Mark started *pushing* and she braced herself and pushed back, in turn, he arched forward and then there was a sudden rush as the head of his cock *popped* inside her ass.

'Oh, *fuck*,' she cried, clamping down, her eyes shut.

She had two men inside her at the same time, and it felt *divine*.

Chapter Six

She looked up at Amy as Mark slowly began to thrust, her eyes widening and her mouth falling open. '*Fuck,*' she said again and moaned.

The feeling was powerful and intense and she had never felt more *wanted* as all of their hands ran across her body, and up her thighs, and around her tummy, and over her back.

The men had to get into a rhythm to make it work, Cassian thrusting up as Mark pulled back, and then Cassian pulling down as Mark thrust in, and after a few more seconds she began to get the hang of the motion.

Then suddenly, almost as soon as they had started, Emilia could feel herself beginning to climax. It was building up from a long way off, like a tsunami. She could feel it gathering strength. It was *different*, centred in another place, and with every thrust, it was getting closer and closer. She couldn't help it now, her moans were no longer just moans, they were primal and *deep* and she could feel both men inside her, growing and pulsing, desperate to come again. They were working for it, their cocks feeling *thick* as though they were going to burst.

She felt full.

Full and more complete than she ever had before, and her mind swam with pleasure.

She gripped Amy's head with her free hand and kissed her so hard she wondered later if she'd hurt her.

Cassian came first, filling her with his love, and Mark came a moment later, her ass radiating his warmth as he shot his seed deep inside her. She could *feel* it, more than she ever could inside her pussy, squirting up and into her.

And then that was it - she fell over the edge.

First, she went silent, and then her whole body *quivered* and *shook*. She could feel Mark inside her bottom, Cassian inside her pussy, Amy *inches* from her face. Then she couldn't feel them at all, as if her body was no longer hers.

And finally, there was nothing but silence and bliss.

Heaven.

Then she heard what sounded like a kettle boiling and realised it was coming from her own mouth as the world filled with colour again and she collapsed forward into Amy, who held her there between her breasts, her arms wrapped tight around her head. - holding her, stroking her, *kissing* her.

They cuddled for a long time as her breathing settled, then Amy shuffled backwards and let her friend flop down on top of Cassian. A moment later she knelt up and kissed Mark as he collapsed down beside her and for a while, they all lay still, *together*.

Cassian cuddling Emilia, Amy cuddling her, Mark cuddling Amy.

They had done it, she thought to herself as she drifted off to sleep, still smiling. They had done it, and it was *perfect*.

Time passed as they all dozed together, drifting in and out of blissful, hazy sleep.

Amy was the first to stand up, but she could barely manage it. Her legs were like jelly, and in the darkness, she grabbed for Emilia's hand.

'Come with me,' she whispered, laughing. 'I'm not sure I'll make it on my own.'

Emilia stirred and smiled and then sat upright, rubbing her eyes. Both the men were still asleep and Cassian was snoring gently.

Together they wobbled to the bathroom, helping each other along, still buzzing with excitement and nervous energy.

Emilia reached the toilet first, so Amy sat herself over the edge of the bath, before immediately leaping up and squealing at how cold it was, but before she could make too much noise, Emilia shushed her and held her hand tight as

Chapter Six

she grabbed a towel and sat back down.

'Oh my fucking *goodness*,' she laughed, leaning forward, her head in her hands. 'This has been the *best* night of my life.'

She peered up at Emilia through splayed fingers, who burst into quiet laughter as she peed. 'Mine too,' she said.

Amy leaned forward and kissed her.

'You know you're kissing me whilst I'm peeing right?' she said through Amy's muffled lips.

'I don't care,' said Amy, kissing her harder as she wrapped her arms around her girl's head, then she reached back and handed her a few pieces of folded toilet paper, and after a little shuffling, they swapped over.

'Thank you,' said Amy.

'What for?'

'For making this happen, for fighting for it, and for being honest.'

Emilia smiled. 'I'm not sure I was *entirely* upfront.'

'I really like you,' said Amy, and then with a softer voice she said. 'Maybe more than that.'

'Me too,' said Emilia, biting her lip as she felt her cheeks glow.

'And Cass,' said Amy.

'And Mark,' smiled Emilia, returning Amy's earlier favour with a small piece of neatly folded toilet roll before the two girls stood to wash their hands.

They looked at themselves in the mirror, their hair mussed up, their naked bodies flushed and tired, red-faced and jelly legged and they laughed and held each other tight as they kissed and kissed. Then they both crept back into the bedroom and slipped onto the bed between their sleeping men, curling up together as a single unit.

Complete, at last.

* * *

Brianna Skylark

*

EPILOGUE

Emilia woke up in a state of perfect bliss. She was warm, the air smelt fresh and bright, and she felt happy and safe, and could hear the relaxing sound of beautiful bird song outside the window, and not a hint of anything else.

She had no regrets.

Everything about last night had been perfect, and for now, nothing was missing. She felt like she had found her *Duke* and her *Duchess*.

She was cuddled up to both Cassian and Amy, and Mark lay asleep spooning his wife - and now *her* girlfriend, at least she *hoped* - beside them.

And they were all still naked.

Amy stirred and smiled, her eyes blurry and heavy, the two of them side by side, facing each other on the pillow, their hair touching, their noses close together.

For a long time, they just looked at one another, then after a while, Emilia started to cry happy tears, and Amy reached out with a thumb and brushed one away from her cheek.

'I don't want this to end,' said Emilia softly. 'I want you both to be with us.'

Amy leaned forward and kissed her sweetly on the lips. It was tender this time, not hard or lustful, but soft and kind and meaningful.

'I don't want this to end either,' she said, and the two of them kept kissing as they smiled

Cassian began to stir next, squinting like a mole, and before long he sat up in the bed, rubbing his eyes and then looking down at the two girls, their bodies embracing each other, their lips locked, and he smiled wide.

'I could get used to this.'

Mark woke now at the sound of his new friend's voice, and rolled over, shielding his eyes from the sun, shining in through the window.

'What? Fucking each other's wives? *Me too*,' he laughed.

The girls kept on kissing affectionately between them as they laughed, Amy raising her middle finger at the pair of them, as she stifled a giggle of her own.

Mark stood up a moment later and scratched his leg. 'I need to pee, but when I get back we're going again.'

Amy stopped kissing Emilia, paling at his commanding voice and then as she rolled over, she smiled. 'Is that a promise?'

He nodded and then looked at Cassian and Emilia. 'You want to warm her up?'

Emilia, who was way ahead of her husband, straddled Amy quickly, her breasts dangling in her face as she grabbed the lube off the bedside table, turning back to face Cassian.

'You're going to need this,' she laughed, handing it to him as Amy gasped. Then quick as a shot, she slid down the bed, parting her girlfriend's thighs with the palms of her hand and kissing her pussy with open lips.

Epilogue

Amy cried out and arched her back, one hand gripping hold of the backboard of the bed and the other finding the top of Emilia's head as her tongue lapped against her opening, savouring the taste and suckling on her clit.

Then satisfied she sat up and licked her lips and watched as her new friend's green eyes turned down to look at her, her chin wet and shining, then she slipped a single finger inside and began to massage her gently as her eyes widened, a soft moan escaping her mouth.

'I mean it you know,' she said, looking up into Amy's large, green and beautiful eyes. 'I don't want this to end.'

'Then let's make sure it doesn't,' whispered Amy, quivering.

And Emilia smiled.

THE END

Keep reading for a sample chapter of the continued adventures of Emilia, Cassian, Amy and Mark in **Play With Us - An Urban Foursome Game Night Fantasy**

Emilia's favourite book **The Paramour - A Romantic Victorian Ménage** is also available to own on **Kindle** or read for free on **Kindle Unlimited.**

PLAY WITH US - SAMPLE CHAPTER

Emilia woke up and smiled.

The fresh smell of a beautiful spring morning drifted in through the open window as soft shafts of golden sunlight shone brightly between the slatted blinds hung in the frame. Motes of dust drifted in the beams like dandelion seeds floating on the breeze as she yawned and stretched, tucking the duvet up to her neck and snuggling back into it.

Her husband Cassian lay beside her, still lost in the depths of a deep and gentle slumber. His large, muscular frame dwarfed her own and she loved how small he made her feel when he wrapped his arms around her.

She rolled onto her side and watched him sleeping. Sometime in the night, he'd pushed the covers away and they'd bunched around his waist, revealing his toned and muscular olive-skinned chest. He was so handsome, and looking at him like this made her whole body *ache* with desire.

She listened and watched as his chest rose and fell. The gentle, sweet sound of his light snoring was soothing and if he was away, travelling to see clients, she would often struggle to get to sleep without hearing him snuffling away during the night.

His beard was soft and dark and she couldn't resist reaching out and stroking it with the back of her hand. At her touch, he rolled onto his side and sniffed and then mumbled something in his sleep.

A shiver of arousal ran through her. She'd been dreaming about something *naughty*.

She frowned as she tried to remember what it was, but each time she felt like she was within finger-tip touching distance of grasping it, the memory slipped further away. It was like it was alive and evading her and the more she woke up, the more nimble it became.

Then suddenly she had it, and it all flooded back.

She'd been dreaming about her naughty book again. About the Duke and his lover, the Duchess Elizabeth and *her* lover, Lady Victoria. Except in her dream, she was Victoria and her new friend Amy, was the Duchess.

Tingling with excitement at the visions of her dream, Emilia quietly and slowly brushed her fingers across her own breast and then down beneath the covers, closing her eyes.

They had been walking in the wild gardens of the Duke's manor, past harebells and callunas, primroses and thistles, along a sculpted bordered edge which wound its way through the uneven grounds and across a little wooden bridge above a gentle brook.

Emilia slipped her hand inside her knickers and began to touch herself as quietly as she could.

As they'd walked their fingers had brushed gently against one another, with neither one wanting to reach out and hold the other's hand for fear of accusations of impropriety. But as they'd neared the bridge, the Duchess had run ahead of her and leaned over the side before looking back and smiling.

'No one is around,' she'd said as she'd approached. '*Kiss* me.'

Taken aback, she'd turned around in shock, afraid that one of the gardeners may have heard *Her Grace's* advance.

Emilia quickened her pace, opening her eyes briefly to check that Cassian was still asleep.

Satisfied that the immediate vicinity of the garden was devoid of the presence of prying eyes, she'd stepped closer and embraced her secret lover, but as soon as their soft warm lips had met they'd heard the hard crunch of approaching feet on the gravel path.

The Duke's feet.

The covers had fallen further away as she'd pleasured herself and she glanced down now and saw in surprise that Cassian's *gloriously* hard member was poking out through the fly of his tight black boxers. The tip glistened in the morning light and she wondered for a moment what kind of dream *he* was having.

A naughty idea crossed her mind. A *really* naughty idea.

She rolled over onto her side, facing away from him and then slipped off her knickers and pushed them down to the bottom of the mattress with her feet. He'd ask her on so many occasions to wake him up like this and *now* seemed like the perfect, serendipitous opportunity.

Slowly and with a delicate ease, she slid herself across the bed towards him, parting her thighs and reaching her hand between her legs as she approached his straining member. Her fingers touched the tip a second later, and she felt him *surge* and grow, then she looked over her shoulder and smiled when she saw that his eyes were still closed.

Carefully she bit down her lip, and slipped the palm of her hand around him as gently as she could, shifting herself another few inches closer until the throbbing tip of his cock pressed firmly against her now soaking wet opening, just as the Duke had done in her dream only moments before she'd woken up - *her skirts pushed up around her waist, her body pressed up against the little wooden bridge, holding the hand of the Duchess as he had thrust inside her* - then she felt him twitch and shift and she *froze*.

Ever so slowly she looked back over her shoulder.

He had stirred, but once again, he hadn't woken. It was now or never.

She lined him up, pressing him between her lips with her fingers and then *pushed* backwards.

She gasped as he entered her, his huge warm length sliding through her entrance with such ease it made her dizzy, and she kept pushing until he was all the way inside, then she paused and waited.

She could feel him twitching and quivering, like a long slow and rhythmic pulse.

She lay still, not daring to move.

It felt *so* good.

She wasn't sure if he was still asleep or not, but she couldn't hold back any longer. She pulled forward, feeling the shape of his head inside her as it slid along her sweet canal, then she pushed back again, thrusting him up inside her.

A moment later, she felt his hand feel its way around her hip, his fingers gripping her skin, then he rolled her onto her front, pinning her down with such ease that it made her feel dizzy, and she bit her lip and smiled.

'*Morning*,' she said blushing hard as he *sank* his cock into her so deep that she moaned into the pillow.

'Morning,' he whispered in her ear.

Emilia gripped the bed sheets and squeezed her thighs together as he began to make love to her in earnest, turning her head to one side, her eyes still closed. 'Were you dreaming about Amy?' she whispered, softly.

Cassian's cock surged inside of her, as though the tip had grown and pulsed, as though he was about to come from just the *mention* of the girl he'd made love to barely two nights ago, and instantly he slowed down and she grinned.

'I'll take that as a *yes*.'

'*Maybe*,' he laughed, pushing himself up onto his muscular arms. His pace increased again a heartbeat later and she saw that he was looking down, watching his cock sliding in and out of her, just below the cheeks of her bottom.

It was the first time that they'd made love since they'd spent the night with their new friends Mark and Amy two days before. Prior to the weekend, Emilia had *never* been with anyone else but her husband. No other man had ever been inside her, until Mark. Cassian too had never been with another woman until he'd made love to Amy on the same bed.

Now her husband was back inside her, and it felt like he was *reclaiming* her. He felt passionate, strong and urgent. His left hand slid down her spine affectionately and came to a rest on her bottom, his fingers playing across her cheeks as he made her his again. Suddenly he leaned forward and whispered in her ear. 'Did you like it when Mark's cock was in your ass?'

She squirmed in embarrassment and buried her face in the pillow. Then nodded.

'How did it feel?'

She turned her head sideways as Cassian pushed deep into her again. 'Good,' she said, quietly, then even quieter. '*Naughty*.'

'Did he come inside you?'

She nodded again, a quiet moan escaping her lips as she did.

'Did it feel good?'

'*Uh-huh*,' she moaned, reaching up and holding his cheek in her palm. 'Harder.'

Cassian obliged.

'*Yes*,' she whispered, laying her arm flat again and gripping hold of the sheets as his muscle-bound body bore down onto her, stretching her pussy with his growing cock.

'Do you want him to fuck you again?'

'Yes,' she said even louder.

'Say it,' said Cassian.

'I want Mark to *fuck* me,' she said.

'Where?'

'*Everywhere*,' she said, crying out now.

She was going to come, like an avalanche crashing down the side of a mountain, there was no stopping it. *She was boiling over.* As she climaxed she went silent, her eyes screwed shut and her mouth wide open as Cassian continued to plough into her from behind.

A heartbeat later she saw stars as her fingers and toes tingled and spread out, curling and flexing. Then she began to shake and throb, and suddenly Cassian pulled out of her, and she fell forward, coiling into a tight ball as the powerful orgasm wracked her body. She shook and breathed and moaned and *twitched*, as wave after wave of pleasure spread throughout her body.

Then Cassian was pulling her up again and rolling her over.

He wasn't done.

She felt weak and wobbly, and barely able to move and as she looked back at him she saw that he was still hard, and she grinned.

Slowly, she sat upright and shuffled towards him, taking his manhood in her palm and sliding her hand up and down it *once* as she brought it close to her mouth, letting it touch the edge of her lips.

Teasing him.

Then she took him in as deep as she could, running her tongue over his head and slowing down to look up at him, his eyes meeting hers with such love and affection that hers filled with tears for a moment.

'I love you,' he whispered..

She slid him further into her, going as far as she could manage into her throat and then she rocked back and forth whilst looking up, her fingers closed tight around his shaft.

She could tell he was going to come fast, so she *sped up*, squeezing her lips around him as his stomach tightened, his abs popping and straining, then she reached up and cupped him as he groaned, and a moment later she felt him retract and *pulse* as her mouth filled with his warm seed.

She melted as she felt him *pumping* into her throat, sliding him back and forth, teasing every last drop out of him as he buckled.

She loved doing this to him. She *loved* making his knees go weak. She loved *him*.

A moment later he toppled forward onto the bed beside her and she lay down resting her head on his chest, feeling and listening to it rise and fall, slower and slower as he recovered. His whole body was covered in a sheen of sweat and Emilia found it intoxicating, as though it was a pheromone that she couldn't resist.

She found herself getting aroused again. It was as though making love with Amy and Mark had sparked some animal instinct in them both. Something *primal*. A powerful urge to reclaim each other, but it wasn't driven by jealously. It was driven by love and lust.

'I love you too,' she said, looking at up him.

Without opening his eyes, Cassian leaned down and kissed her on the top of the head.

Emilia turned, still wrapped inside the warm embrace of his arm, and looked across to the window. The sun had risen higher into the sky and the golden light of the morning was brightening into daylight. Out across the garden, she could see a fine mist drifting through the trees. It reminded her of the morning they had arrived at the spa, an how the drive over through the valley, filled with clouds and mist, had been so beautiful. How the trees by the pool had felt mysterious. How it had made her feel isolated, yet safe.

The morning after, they'd all made love again.

All of them together.

Then they'd breakfasted and parted ways, but since then, they had heard nothing.

Amy hadn't called or texted, and she and Cassian hadn't talked about it until just now.

It was as though it hadn't happened.

Emilia didn't want that.

'Did you like making love with them?' she said timidly, her fingers idly playing with the hair on her husband's chest.

He breathed deeply, Emilia's head rising and falling with each breath, then he reached up and smoothed his hand over her long blonde hair, running his fingers through the soft strands.

'Yes,' he said.

Emilia looked up at him excitedly smiling. 'Really?'

He nodded. 'Of course.'

'What did it feel like... being with Amy?'

He blinked and hesitated. 'Different.'

'I don't want you to feel like this is some shitty trap I'm leading you into, I really want to know.'

He looked into his wife's eyes and smiled, reassured. 'She felt amazing,' he said.

'Did you like her pussy?' she grinned. 'Did she feel really good?'

He nodded, smiling. 'How did Mark feel?'

'*Thick*,' she said.

'Thick?' he frowned.

Emilia nodded. 'He's girthier than you. You're longer, he's thicker.'

As she spoke her fingers worked their way down his chest and across his abdomen.

'What did it feel like when we were both inside you?' he asked.

'Warm and *full*,' she said as she buried her face in his chest, her fingers still moving down towards his crotch. 'I can't believe we're talking about this.'

Cassian leaned down and kissed her on the lips as her fingertips danced across his hardening member. 'I liked watching you with him,' he said, quietly. 'I liked watching you come.'

She blushed and looked away, feeling suddenly awkward, almost ashamed. 'Even though it wasn't you?'

He shrugged. 'I like seeing you happy, it makes *me* feel happy.'

'*You* make me happy,' she said as she closed her fingers around him and looked up.

'It helped that I was inside Amy at the time,' he laughed. 'I reckon that *eased* the jealously a little.'

'You felt jealous?' she said, as she began to slide her hand up and down his shaft.

'Yes, and no,' he said. 'I don't feel jealous now though.'

'Do you want to see them again?' she felt him harden at the suggestion.

'Yes.'

'Would you like to make love with them again?'

'*Yes*,' he said. His cock was full now and throbbing in her hand.

'Do you want to fuck *Amy* again?' she started to slide up

and down faster now as Cassian lay his head back on the pillow and closed his eyes.

'*Uh-huh,*' he moaned.

'I liked watching you with her. When she lay down flat, and you fucked her from behind? I liked seeing her face as she came,' she breathed deeply and smiled. 'And I liked watching you come *inside her.*'

She felt him shake and sigh, and as she continued to stroke him, she rolled over and opened her bedside drawer, pulling out a small object and holding it tight in her free hand. 'You know,' said Emilia. 'You're, *once again,* the last man to fuck me...' Cassian opened his eyes and looked across at her, confused as she continued. 'But *Mark,* was the last man to fuck my *ass.*'

Her husband's eyes widened as Emilia slipped the small bottle of lube into his hands.

'Shall we change that?' she said, grinning as she rolled over and lay on her front.

Cassian was up like a shot and she listened, grinning as he unscrewed the little bottle before looking back as he began to hurriedly coat himself in the slick liquid.

'I'm all yours,' she smiled, as he quickly knelt behind her.

His throbbing cock looked as hard as a steel girder as he placed his hands on her cheeks, and a moment later she gasped as she felt the tip of his cock pressing gently against her sweet little hole.

Then she bit down on her bottom lip and whispered. 'Please, *be gentle,*' but she knew that was a lie...

Want more? Treat yourself to a little alone time...

Buy it now on Kindle or read it for free on Kindle Unlimited

* * *

Brianna Skylark

*

THANK YOU

Thank you for reading **Be With Us!**

You can now **rate my books without leaving a review on Amazon**, but if you do have a few moments to spare, I'd love to hear your thoughts.

Even just a couple of lines makes a **HUGE** difference, and I would be so grateful. It really helps other amazing readers like yourself feel *confident* in giving a **new author a try.**

If you have the time to rate it, or leave a review on Goodreads or BookBub too, that would be incredible!

Follow me on Amazon, Twitter, Instagram, Goodreads & BookBub

Subscribe to my newsletter for all my latest news, new

releases and deals!

Read the #1 Bestselling Fantasy Swingers series

Innocent wife Elsie can't get enough of her **rugged and insatiable** husband Cole. But there are some things that are **off-limits, filthy...** *taboo.*

So when Cole accidentally touches her in her **most private and untouched place**, it shakes the very foundations of their marriage, leaving her desperate for more. Her newfound kink has Elsie questioning everything, including her shameful crush on her best friend Alice.

Now that **nothing is off the table** and their darkest fantasies are out in the open, can their blissful marriage survive? Or will **temptation and desire** tear them apart for good?

*'This was my **first**, and **definitely not last** read of Brianna Skylark... what are you trying to **DO** to me?!* **THAT. WAS. HOT!!!**

★★★★★

*'This story is a **real breath of fresh air**. This is **super** sexy erotica. Careful where you read this one, folks!'*

★★★★★

* * *

*'Sensual, **stimulating**, seductive, beautiful and written with love. You can feel every push, every stretch!*

★★★★★

Read the *number one bestselling series* on Kindle & Kindle Unlimited

Read the #1 Bestselling First Time Swingers anthology series

Each tale explores the lives of two fresh couples as they experience a whole new lifestyle of passion and indulgence for the very first time.

In **Into the Swing**, Freya and Cameron meet Ash and Naomi, a gorgeous working couple who turn their lives upside down in one desperate and passion filled night that just might change everything… forever.

In **Back Swing**, Ashleigh and Claire and their husbands Noah and Jay, engage in an explosive game of truth or dare as they head to the sauna.

And in **Hot Swing**, Elina and Antonio invite Callie and Jack over for a night of fun and games in their brand new hot tub…

And in **Mistletoe Swing**, a married couple share a lot more than a cheeky Christmas vacation in New York when they visit some old friends for some festive fun…

Whatever your flavour, you're in for a delicious treat. From the highlands to the big city, experience what it's like to take that first step, and push the boundaries of monogamy into a realm of pleasure, beauty and quivering bliss.

'In my top five in the erotica genre! So good that I don't know how to review it!'

★★★★★

Amazon Review

Read the rest of my brand new anthology series now on Kindle & Kindle Unlimited

Read the #1 Bestselling The Billionaire's Naked Cleaner Series

A mysterious billionaire, a shy hipster chick and a rebellious playboy hacker.

Sophie is broke, single and jobless. She's two weeks away from eviction and is facing the very real possibility of having to move back in with her country bumpkin parents. Then her best friend makes a throwaway comment that changes her life forever…

One day later and she's setup her own cleaning business, Sweet and Discreet. It's a one girl cleaning service with a naked twist.

Three clients, three very different encounters. All of them want her and with each sparkling visit, the tension escalates, surely it's only a matter of time before squeaky-clean Sophie gets down on her hands and knees… for some dirty fun.

*'WOW! This builds from teasing to sensual, to downright **scorching**.'*

★★★★★

Read the *number one bestselling series* on Kindle & Kindle

Unlimited, and follow Sophie as her high-end client list quickly grows. With each new skin-tingling encounter becoming naughtier than the last, will she maintain her composure and remain professional… or will she succumb to temptation, curiosity and **raw naked attraction?**

ABOUT THE AUTHOR

BRIANNA SKYLARK is the pen name of a happily married, utterly insatiable, thirty-something mother of two living in a repressed little village on the south coast of England.

She's the wife of a rugged archeologist and often likes to think she's married to Indiana Jones. Over the years she's experimented with various occupations including filmmaking, video game voiceover artist and climbing instructor, but her favourite job is her most recent one... steamy romance novelist.

She loves bringing sweet, strong, faithful and loving women to life through her books, and then introducing them to strong, kind and endearing alpha males (or sensual females) who satisfy their every desire in the bedroom and beyond.

When she's not writing, she's often found hiking or climbing in the far reaches of Scotland and Wales or exploring the woods and beaches near her home with the man of her dreams, and their two gorgeous children.

Follow me on Amazon, Twitter, Instagram, Goodreads & BookBub

www.briannaskylark.com
Short, secret, sexy and sweet.

Printed in Great Britain
by Amazon